Copyright © DL Gallie 2020

Falling for Dr. Knight

First published 3rd June 2020

Email: dlgallieauthor@outlook.com

Edited by **Karen Hrdlicka**, Barren Acres Editing

Cover by **Kristie**, Vanilla Lily Design

Proofread by **Lana Clarke** and **Margaret Neal**

Andi, Preston is all yours.
Thank you for believing in him, and me.

"Love until it hurts. Real love is always painful and hurts:
then it's real and pure"
     ~ *Mother Teresa*

PROLOGUE

When I saw my daughter in the ER bed getting stitched up after the accident at Navy Pier, I thought that was the worst possible thing to happen to me, but hearing, "Cress, Lexi has sepsis," **THAT** was the most heartbreaking thing a mother could hear. And to kick me even more when I was down, let's also add, "She has now developed pneumonia." Even with the bad news coming from the man I'm in love with, it did nothing to cushion the blow. Seeing the seriousness on his face was when I broke down. I realized in that moment just how sick my little girl was.

She was sick, really really sick; and he wouldn't promise me that she'd get better.

When Preston said those words my world imploded. After the initial shock wore off, the guilt set in. I felt like the worst mother in the entire universe, add in threats from Dickwad Dawson and the already stressful situation became even more volatile. *Fuck my life.* I should have known that life would fuck me over. Things were going smoothly and for the first time since Lexi was born, I was happy, ecstatically happy and in love. But with this kick in the guts, I didn't know if I could fix it. I wasn't a wizard, I couldn't wave my magic wand or cast a spell like Twilight Sparkle to make Lexi healthy again. My little girl, my most precious possession, was sick and it was all my fault. I should have seen the signs. I should have paid more attention. I shouldn't have been fucking around with Preston. I should have been focusing on Lexi. I should have been there for her.

I.

Should.

Have.

Known.

I'm her mom for fuck's sake! How could I have let my little girl down so badly? I should have noticed the color draining from her face. I should have seen how lethargic she'd become. I should have brought her in sooner. I should have done more. I should have been a better mom.

And now because I was following my heart, my little girl is close to death. The apple of my eye is fighting for her life and it's all my fault. Falling for Dr. Knight was the worst thing I've ever done.

1 CRESS

...five years earlier

NEVER HAVE I FELT PAIN LIKE THIS BEFORE, NOT EVEN WHEN Creed walked away while I was pregnant. That day was hard, but this, this is the hardest thing I have ever done. "Avery, get me drugs. Get me every fucking drug there is. It hurts so much," I scream and cry to my best friend, who has stepped up to the plate and takes the crown as THE bestest friend ever in the history of best friends.

"If you let go of my hand, I will see what I can do," she says through clenched teeth. I loosen the grip I have on her hand, and when she pulls it away, she shakes it back and forth, stretching her fingers, and then shaking again to get the blood flow back into it.

"I'm sorry," I cry and then I burst into tears. "Avery, I'm going to be a shit mom," I blubber. "I just squished your hand. What if I squish the baby? I can't do this on my own."

"Cressida Rachel Bayliss, stop talking shit—"

"But—" I try to interrupt her, but she raises her hand in a stop motion. I know she means business because not only did she middle name me, she full named me too.

"Don't make me bitch slap a pregnant woman in labor. You've got this. You are the strongest most amazing person I know, and this baby will be lucky to have you as his or her mommy."

"Avery," I cry, tears well in my eyes and then the dam breaks. Tears pour down my face but this time instead of fearful tears, they are happy emotional tears. "You're not meant to make a pregnant lady in labor cry."

"Well, stop talking shit and I won't. Now let me go find the nurse, or Dr. Jenkins, and get you some drugs."

"I knew you were my best friend for a reason." I mean every word in that statement. Ave is my ride or die. She's my best bitch and I would be lost without her.

After my mini freak-out, Munchkin—the affectionate term I used while pregnant with her—yes, her—came quickly, like super quick. She announced her arrival into the world with a scream to rival that of Jamie Lee Curtis in *Halloween*. I'm pretty sure I was a close second with the screaming, because pushing a nine-pound baby out your hoo-ha is no easy feat. Alexis Avery Bayliss, or Lexi for short, arrived before I could get the good drugs, but as soon as they put her in my arms, everything was right with the world. The pain of the labor vanished. All my fears of being a shitty mom disappeared. I was filled with love, awe, and gratitude. My daughter is the most perfect beautiful baby in the world, I know all parents say this but in regards to Lexi, it's true.

For a brief moment, I thank Dickwad Dawson for knocking me up because if he hadn't, I wouldn't be holding my beautiful little girl in my arms right now. Guess I better let him know she has arrived, not that he'll care. My mind drifts to the day I told him I was pregnant and the events that unfolded after that...

...Sitting on the side of the tub, I look down at the four sticks sitting on the floor mat and the one in my hand. All I see are pink lines staring back up at me screaming 'You're pregnant!,' insert jazz hands. A smile breaks free. "I'm pregnant," I murmur and rest my hand on my belly. "Hey, Munchkin, I'm your mommy. I'm promise to be the bestest mommy in the world."

The sound of the front door closing startles me and I drop the stick I'm holding.

"Cress, Babydoll, where are you?" Creed shouts, as I hear his boots hit the wall by the door. I hate when he kicks his shoes off like that.

"In here," I shout, as I turn on the faucet and wash my hands to get rid of the residual pee. Creed walks in and smiles at me in the mirror. I stare at his reflection. Brown hair. Brown eyes. Square jaw. I start to wonder what our baby will look like. Since I have dark blonde, almost brown hair, I guess she, or he, will have dark hair too. I have blue eyes so it's anyone's guess. Our skin tone is similar. But my thoughts and happiness are thwarted when I hear him growl, "What the fuck?"

Shaking my head, I turn around to see him glaring at the pile of pregnancy tests on the bathroom floor. "Surprise," I say, but when I look at his face, I don't see excitement or awe. I see anger, rage, and disgust.

"You need to get rid of it," he snarls between clenched teeth. I have never heard that tone from him before. "I'm not ready to be a father, and you certainly aren't in any shape to be a mother.

You can't even boil a fucking egg without calling Mommy for assistance."

"Excuse me?" I scoff, I'm shocked at the outburst coming from him right now.

"You heard me. Me no father and you no mom." He pauses. "Hell, it's probably not even mine."

"Excuse me?" I shout again. "How dare you accuse me of cheating on you! I have been nothing but an amazing girlfriend. Sure, the timing isn't ideal but we'll make this work. I know we can. We will be a happy family."

"Yeah, we will because you're going to get rid of it."

"Ummm, no, I'm not."

"Yes. You. Are," he growls, pausing between each word for emphasis. His face turning purple from holding his breath. I can feel the anger radiating from him but I refuse to let him ruin the moment. This is a joyous time for me. For us. For our future.

"No, Creed. I'm keeping this baby. We made Munchkin together, he or she is going to be perfect and we will be amazing parents."

"Fuck this shit." He punches the mirror, the glass cracking and splintering under the force. He turns around and walks out, leaving me stunned. He turns back around. "You need to think who you want more, me? Or that thing?" He points to my belly and before I can reply, he's gone. Leaving me alone with Munchkin and my heart broken.

Dropping to my knees, I cry. My happy moment and life crushed by the one person who I thought would be by my side forever. When I have no more tears left to cry, I lean back against the tub and cradle my stomach. I look down at my flat for now abs and whisper, "I'll choose you every time, Munchkin, every time."

A few hours later, Creed returns and he drops to the floor in front of me. He takes my hands in his and lovingly stares at me.

"I'm sorry, Babydoll. I was shocked, it was so out of the blue. I don't want you to get rid of it—"

"Munchkin." I say, smiling at him, "Our lil' munchkin is growing inside of me." Taking his hand, I place it on my belly and stare at him. "I love you, Creed. We are going to be fine, and this baby is going to have two amazing parents, sure we'll fumble, but together, we can do anything."

"I'll try, Babydoll, but I'm scared."

"I'm scared too, baby, but together, we can do this. We can be a family."

For the next few weeks everything was perfect, then one night he came home drunk. He wanted to fool around but I've been suffering from horrible morning sickness, so much for that disappearing in the second trimester. He got angry when I said no. "Fucking baby is cockblocking me already. Knew it was going to mess with us. I thought pregnancy made you bitches horny all the time. Knew you should have gotten rid of it."

"Not this again," I mumble, but it was obviously louder than I intended because he slapped me across the face. Cupping my cheek in shock, I stare at the man before me. He isn't the man I fell in love with all those years ago.

"Don't sass me, woman. I knew this baby was a mistake, you not putting out proves that."

He climbs off the bed and leaves, slamming the door behind him. It was three days before he returned home. He never told me where he disappeared to, and to be honest, I didn't care.

This pregnancy has been tough; I've been so sick this past week. Thankfully I have Avery and Mom to help me. Between the two of them, I've had round the clock care. The topic of Creed is never bought up, and I'm thankful for that because I don't know what to say.

When he finally came home, it all went back to normal, well for the next few weeks anyway. The day of our twenty week scan, he didn't turn up, to say I was hurt was an understatement. When I got home, that hurt intensified. I found him packing.

"What's going on?"

"I'm leaving. I can't do this. I can't be a father to that thing." He points to my bump and scowls. "I'm still not convinced that thing is mine anyway, so I'm leaving."

At his words, my heart and world shatter. Tears well in my eyes. "But—"

"There's no buts, I'm gone. You will always chose that thing over me. I'm worth more than that, if you can't see that then there's no point in me hanging around."

"Please, Creed," I beg, "Please don't leave us." Tears pour down my face as the man I love continues to pack.

He stops packing and looks at me. "Get rid of it and I'll stay."

"You know I won't do that. I can't do that."

"Then I'm gone."

"You said you love me! That you'd try. That we'd be a family."

He breaks out into a sarcastic laugh. "Love you? That's a good one, Cress. You said all the happily ever after shit, not me." He zips up his suitcase and walks toward me. He stops and cups my face in his palm. "It's such a shame, you were such a good fuck." He taps my cheek and walks past me.

"You said you wanted to try, remember? You said you'd be here, for us. For our child."

He turns to face me. "I said I'd try for you, not that thing. I still don't even know if it's mine." He pauses. "You had your chance, Cress, and even now, you're still choosing it over me. You chose wrong, Babydoll." He turns around and walks toward the front door. With his hand on the door handle, he looks back at me. "You did this to yourself, Cressida. In a couple of months, you'll be nothing but a fat, pregnant, ugly bitch. Because this *thing you keep calling munchkin is going to steal everything from you and give you nothing in return." With those hateful words, he opens the door and walks out. Leaving me pregnant, alone, and completely heartbroken…*

The door to my room opens and snaps me back to the present and away from that fateful day. A group of doctors enters for rounds, thankfully this only happens twice a day, I cannot wait to go home where it will just be Lexi and me. Looking up, I smile at Dr. Jenkins and glance around at the other doctors with her. My eyes land on a doctor hiding in the back, holy hotness, Batman, he is the most beautiful man I have ever seen. Then I realize I look like a hot mess. I haven't slept in a gazillion hours and yesterday; I punched a watermelon out my hoo-ha with no drugs. *Why, universe, why would you do this to me?*

"Cressida," the doctor says, and I internally cringe, I *hate* being called Cressida.

Shaking my head, I focus on her. "Sorry, I missed that, Dr. Jenkins?"

"Can we have a quick look at Alexis?"

Dropping my gaze, I look to a sleeping Lexi in my arms and smile. I've been doing that a lot in the last twenty-four hours. She is the apple of my eye and I don't ever want to give her up. "Umm," my voice wavers and I hesitate, "she's just drifted off."

She can see the trepidation in my eyes, but her face softens in that dreamy way it does regarding babies. "That's fine, we can come back later." And that is why I chose Dr. Stefanie Jenkins to deliver my baby: she cares and takes my feelings into account. I was not the easiest of patients, with being a first-time mom and doing it alone, but she was my savior.

Before I can say anything the group exits my room. Dr. Hottie is the last to leave, our eyes connect and the moment could not be more perfect. It's intense. It's electric. His gaze penetrates deep into my soul, my skin heats as his eyes roam over me. He winks and turns to leave. Looking over his shoulder, he says, "Congrats on the birth of your little girl, Cress."

"Thank you," I manage to utter as the door closes behind him.

He called me Cress, it's like he knew I hate being called Cressida. And his voice, ohh my God, his voice. It's deep and husky, I could listen to him talk all day long. Hell, I'd even listen to him read the phone book. Lex stirs in my arms and I realize I need to pee. I shuffle out of bed and I place her in the bassinet in my room. After using the bathroom, I climb back into bed, and drift off to sleep, dreaming about Dr. Hottie.

After that morning, I never saw Dr. Hottie again but it wouldn't have mattered anyway, a guy like him would never go for someone like me. Plus, I don't need a man in my life; I now have a baby to focus on. I'm going to be the best mom ever to my little munchkin.

2 PRESTON

....present day

FLOPPING DOWN ON THE SOFA, I KICK OUT MY LEGS AND FLICK on the TV. Bringing up Disney+, I grin when I see *Duck-Tales* is currently playing. Lying back, I watch as Huey, Dewey, and Louie get into mischief and like usual, Scrooge McDuck is being all scroogey. Drifting off to sleep, I wake up when the alarm on my phone blares, reminding me I need to pick up Flynn from the airport. Thank God I set the reminder because I totally forgot I was to collect him today.

Hopping up, I grab a quick shower and make my way to the airport to pick Flynn up. Lucky bastard has spent the last ten days in paradise at Oasis, an adults-only resort in Castaway Grove. I'm sure on the trip back to his place, I'll hear all about his conquests…ohh how wrong I was. "Are you telling me, Dr. 'I have an accent, drop your panties now' has blue balls and callouses on his hands?"

He nods his head and sighs dejectedly, "Yep."

This is pure gold. The Irish God—according to the nurses, well anyone with a vagina, at the hospital—got cockblocked by the woman of his dreams, and he spent the last few days at the resort by himself, with Mrs. Palmer and her five daughters, watching her douche of an ex swoop in and win her back.

"Sounds like you need to get laid and you need to get laid good."

"Tell me about it. I feel like a teenager again."

"If you like, we can go out tonight," I offer.

He once again shakes his head. "Nah, I need to get home, unpack, and get my head back into the game. Plus, I've got an early shift tomorrow."

"No worries, some other time then."

The rest of the trip to his place is silent. I've never seen Flynn so down, it's concerning, and I kind of feel guilty for the teasing earlier. We pull up to his building. Turning off the car, we climb out and I help him with his bags.

"Thanks for picking me up, man…and the talk."

"Anytime, you know that." Flynn and I met in med school and we hit if off straightaway. And as they say, the rest was history. Our friendship has grown stronger over the years, he's more like a brother than a friend and colleague. I'd do anything for him, and I know he'd do the same for me too.

"Appreciate it. I'll see you tomorrow." We do the manly, one-arm, backslap hug and I watch him walk inside. Shaking my head, I internally laugh at him and his blue balls. Climbing back into my car, I head back home. Stopping along the way, I grab some Chinese and in front of the TV, I watch old-school *Scooby Doo*—hey, I'm a pediatrician and spend all day with kids, plus I'm a big kid at heart—and I eat my sweet and sour chicken, thinking about the busy week ahead.

Friday finally rolls around, this has been the slowest week in history but it did allow me to catch up on paperwork; who knew there'd be so much paperwork being a doctor? I've just finished up a meeting with admin when I get word that Flynn lost a patient earlier this afternoon. I know my friend, he will be gutted and as his best friend it's my duty to cheer him up. Making my way to the doctors' lounge, I walk in and see Flynn sitting in front of his locker. His shoulders are down and he's ignoring everyone, but I won't let him ignore me. "Dude," I say as I walk over to him. When he sees it's me, he stands and greets me with our one-armed man hug, and then he sits back down. "Sorry to hear about your patient."

"Thanks, man." He begins to change out of his scrubs. "How he held on as long as he did is beyond me. There was literally nothing I could have done."

"That's tough," I offer in condolence, there's nothing worse than losing a patient, especially for me since I deal with kids. The death of a child always sucks ass, actually the death of anyone is rough.

Before I get to ask him about heading out for a few drinks, he beats me to it. "Drinks?"

"Hell, yes. It's been a rough week."

"That's putting it mildly."

After changing my shirt, Flynn and I hop into my car and we head to The Fat Fox Tavern. We decide on a bar away from the hospital because if we went to O'Malley's, the one closest to the hospital, the topic of conversation would turn to work and people would offer condolences to Flynn and that's the last thing he needs. Tonight he needs to get drunk and maybe hook up with a chick… giving his palm a rest and ease his blue balls.

We enter the tavern and head toward the bar; my eyes gravitate toward a gorgeous chick sitting at the bar with her friend. Her friend is hot, with blonde hair and blue eyes, but it's the other gorgeous woman I'm intrigued by. She lights up the room when she smiles and her laugh is like music to my ears. I order our drinks and notice Flynn looking in the same direction. I hope, and pray, that he wants the other chick. With our beers in hand, we walk over to a table and silently sit down. Flynn's eyes are still locked on the girls, as are mine, and I'm trying to gauge whom he's checking out.

The goddess I've been admiring looks over to us and that's when I realize Flynn is eyeing her friend. *Thank you,* I silently say to the big guy upstairs. He chugs back his beer and without saying a word, he slams the empty glass on the table, walks back to the bar but this time, he heads over to the girls. My eyes are locked on the dark-haired angel, when suddenly, the friend spins around and hits Flynn in the nuts. I clench my nuts, feeling his pain in my own balls, but I'm also laughing. It was like a scene from a black-and-white slapstick comedy. It's the funniest shit I've seen in a long time, I can't remember the last time I laughed this hard. I watch the scene unfold and shake my head when he smoothly leans in and fucks her mouth in the middle of the tavern. *The Irish fucker has done it again,* I think to myself as I watch him make out with the blonde chick, her friend watching from the sidelines grinning from ear to ear.

Picking up his beer, he walks back toward me with a smug look on his face.

"How's the nuts?" I tease as he takes a seat.

"Now they'll be purple and blue, but if I play my cards right, they won't be blue after tonight." He winks at me and takes a sip of beer.

Shaking my head, I pick up mine and drink. The woman looks to Flynn and he winks at her. I see it written on her face, she's going home with the Irish stallion tonight. Out of nowhere, Flynn slams his glass down—again—and stalks across the bar. "What's he up to?" I mumble to myself, as I watch him walk toward the restrooms, the blonde nowhere in sight.

From the corner of my eye, I see my angel sitting at the bar by herself. She looks over her shoulder and even though we are in a packed bar, our gaze connects. Time stands still. Everything around me disappears, everything except for her. Our eyes are locked on one another. It's intense. It's electric. It feels like déjà vu. Her gaze penetrates deep into my soul, my skin heats as her eyes roam over me. She winks and turns her attention back to the bartender. *Ohh, I'm taking this one home tonight*, I think to myself, as Flynn and her friend walk back into the bar from the restrooms together. Her cheeks are flushed and he looks like the cat who ate the canary, knowing him, he totally just did that. They stop and speak to the friend, Flynn grabs her purse and they head toward me.

"I'm taking Avery home, please make sure her friend gets home safely." He tells me.

"Roger that." I salute him and wink at Avery, her cheeks darken in embarrassment. He drags her out of the tavern, leaving me alone.

Finishing off my drink, I walk over to the friend. "Seems, I've been tasked with getting you home tonight."

"Lucky me, but I don't recall ordering a handsome Uber to get me off...home," she says. *Ohh the sass on this one is on point,* I think to myself as I take the recently vacated stool next to her.

Offering out my hand, I introduce myself, "Preston Knight, handsome Uber guy."

She smirks at my smart-ass remark. "Nice to meet you." She places her hand in mine and shakes. She has a good grip. Strong. Firm, perfect to wrap around my cock. An image of her fingers wrapped around my cock, stroking from base to tip appears in my mind. Her tongue darting out, licking the head before she swallows my shaft to the hilt.

The clearing of a throat snaps my attention away from my dirty thoughts. I see her looking intently at me. "Where did you just go? You drifted off there."

"Nowhere," I say. I'm so glad she cannot see into my dirty, perverted mind right now, or my dick, which is painfully pressing against my zipper right now.

"Can I buy you a drink?"

"Really? That's what you're going with? Friendly advice, you really need to review your flirting strategies."

"How about over a drink you teach me...insert name here."

She eyes me, her gaze roaming all over my body. She brings her drink to her lips, takes a sip, and spins around to face me, leaning on the bar. "Do you think I'll go home with you, just like my friend did with your friend?"

Shrugging my shoulders, I nonchantly say, "Well, my friend's charm clearly impressed your friend..."

"What my friend and your friend do have nothing to do with me."

"So you think I'm a lesser man than Flynn?"

"I didn't say that." She pauses. "So why don't you take a seat, buy me a drink, and we will see what happens. Plus, I'm not ready to leave with my handsome Uber guy yet. You still need to complete lesson 1-0-1 in flirting." She pauses and smiles at me, it lights up her face. "And my name is Cress."

Taking a seat next to her, I signal the bartender. He nods and finishes serving the couple at the other end and walks over to us. "Two more please," I ask him, but my gaze is on Cress, sassy sexy Cress. Even her name is beautiful. "So, Cress, tell me about the woman under this sexy, sassy exterior."

"You tell me what you see," she sasses in reply.

"Well, I see a very attractive, smart woman with a sharp mind and a quick tongue."

She licks her lips seductively, my eyes drop to her tongue and my cock twitches. It wants that tongue licking him. Hell, I want that tongue licking all over me.

"You also need to add to that assessment, the mom of the most amazing daughter, substitute grade school teacher, coffee addict, and wine lover." She pauses, and then adds, "So, it seems my bestie and your bestie are going to bump uglies tonight."

"And what about you, Cress? Do you bump uglies?"

She shakes her head side to side. "Ohh, no, I don't bump uglies." I deflate at hearing this but then she adds, "I'm more of a do the horizontal tango all night long kind of girl." She takes a sip from her beer. "And what about you, Preston, who are you a knight for?"

"I'm a pediatric doctor at Western General, I guess I'm

a knight to my patients. Well, I try to be anyway." I lean into her, my lips hover near her ear, she smells amazing, "I'm eager to learn how to horizontal tango…with you."

Pulling back, I gaze into her blue eyes, noting her breathing has become labored. She swallows deeply and stares intently back at me. That déjà vu feeling hits me again. Reaching up, I brush a tendril of dark blonde hair behind her ear. Running the tip of my finger along her jawline and down her neck, her skin breaks out in goose-bumps, but our moment is interrupted by the ringing of her phone.

3 CRESS

His stare, it feels like I've felt it on me before but that's not possible, he and I are from two very different worlds. He's a doctor, I'm a single mom and substitute school teacher, we never would have crossed paths before, trust me, I'd remember meeting a Channing Tatum look-alike like him. I'm just about to offer to teach him how to horizontal tango when my phone rings, it's Mom's ringtone. "I need to get this," I tell him. Grabbing my phone from my purse, I swipe to answer, "Hey, Mom."

"Hey, Cress. Sorry to bother you—"

"Mom, it's no bother, is Lexi okay?"

"Kinda sorta. I'm not sure."

Her answer causes my eyes to pop wide open. "What's wrong? Is she okay?" Panic sets in that I'm not there for Lexi. Instead, I'm in a bar with a sexy man. I'm a shitty mom.

"She's running a temperature and she's very lethargic, not Lexi like at all. I'm going to take her to the hospital."

I can feel Preston staring at me, he seems concerned too. "There's no need to take her to the hospital, Mom."

"No need? That's crazy, Cress. She needs to see a doctor."

"I said there's no need to get her to the hospital because I *have* the doctor. We'll be there soon. Tell her Mommy is on her way."

I don't wait for Mom to answer, I look to Preston. "We need to get to my mom's, Lex isn't well. I need you."

"You need me, do you?" he playfully teases, but when he sees the worry etched on my face, he nods his head and stands up. "Okay, let's go."

He throws some bills onto the bar for our drinks. He places his hand low on my back and if I wasn't worried about Lexi right now, my body would be thrumming from the ever so light contact with him. We exit the Fat Fox and head over to his car. It's a sleek, silver Aston Martin; it's the perfect car for the sexy doctor. He unlocks it and opens my door for me—such a gentleman—I climb in and admire the interior, and then I remember that Lexi is sick. I need to stop drooling over his car and focus on getting to Mom's and my daughter.

Pulling my belt on, my leg tics and I bite my nail. Now that I'm thinking about Lexi, I'm anxious to get home to my munchkin. Preston starts the car but he doesn't pull out immediately. He reaches over and pulls my hand away from my mouth and gently squeezes.

My eyes snap to his and he smiles. "She's going to be fine, Cress. Now, what's your mom's address?"

Nodding my head, I tell him her address, he punches it into the navigation system and I stare out the window thinking about my little munchkin and what I'm going to find when I get home. When Ave left, I should have left too. I should be a better mom, I need to be there for Lexi. I'm all she's got. Sure, Dickwad Dawson pops in every now and again, but I don't think she really realizes who he is to her, even though she calls him 'Daddy Creed,' which totally pisses him off. Even though he left me, I will never hold him back from seeing his daughter. I keep hoping that one day he will become the father he promised to be before he left, but I think I have a bigger chance of shitting glitter than that ever happening.

We are stopped at a red light and I feel Preston's hand on my thigh, I have no idea how long it's been there. I look down at his hand and then I look over to him. He's staring at me, calm and cool, the complete opposite to how I look and feel right now. "How you doin, love?"

"Worried."

"You need to stop, I know it's easier said than done but if it was super serious, I'm sure your mom would already be at the hospital with her. We will be there soon and then you can see for yourself that she's okay."

Nodding my head, I think over his words but I don't say anything because right at this moment, I don't know that everything is going to be okay. I don't know anything. Until I see Lex for myself, I'll continue to worry and fret.

We pull up at Mom's house and before Preston has even stopped the car, I'm opening the door and climbing out. Racing up the path, I swing open the front door, and step into the living room. My eyes land on Lexi and her head resting on Mom's lap. *My Little Pony* is playing on the TV. Racing over to her, I drop to my knees and press my palm to her forehead, she feels warm. "Hey, Munchkin, you not feeling well?"

She shakes her head. "Mommy, I don't feel good." She starts to cry but the mom in me knows this is a performance cry, not an Oscar winning one, but she is playing it up, that much I can tell.

"Ohh, baby," I coo, lifting her into my arms, I hug her to me. She wraps her arms around my shoulders and I rock us. Kissing her head and rubbing my hand up and down her back, she snuggles into me and I smile.

"Who are you?" I hear Lexi ask, any hint of sickness in her voice gone; the little faker.

Looking over my shoulder, I see Preston standing there. *Man that man is fine,* I think to myself and then it clicks, there's a man in my mom's house and that man isn't Dickwad Dawson.

"I'm Dr. Knight, your mom tells me you don't feel well?" I feel Lex nod her head. "Can I have a look at you?"

"You already are looking at me."

"I'm a doctor, so I can have a look at you as if you are a patient of mine?"

"But you don't have a white coat or a stesascope."

"I see you're sassy just like your mommy."

Glaring at him, I see that he's focused on Lexi. "You don't have to do that, I'm sure she's fine," I say, throwing his words from earlier back at him. My leg begins to cramp, so I stand up. Lexi gripping onto me like a monkey.

"Yes he does, Mom," Lexi says. "He's a doctor, he'll make me all better." She wriggles down and out of my arms. Walking over to Preston, she takes his hand in hers and pulls him farther into the living room. She dramatically lies down on the sofa, resting her feet on Mom's lap and stares up at Preston. *And the Oscar for fake sick daughter goes to Alexis Avery Bayliss.* I shake my head and watch Preston with Lexi.

He steps toward her. "Okay, let's have a look," Preston says, placing his medical bag down on the coffee table. He opens it up and pulls out a stethoscope. He pops it around his neck and then grabs a digital thermometer. He places it on Lexi's forehead, when it beeps I peer over this shoulder and sigh in relief when I see 99.9° reflecting back at me. "A little high but I'd say it's fine," he confirms, looking at me over his shoulder. The look on his face is calm, cool, and collected, the complete opposite to how I'm feeling. Turning his attention back to Lex, he checks her pulse and nods.

"Can I have a quick listen to your chest?"

"How will you do that?" she asks, I'm sure more questions will follow.

"With this," he says, lifting the stethoscope from his neck.

"I thought a stesascope listens to your heart?"

Preston nods. "It does. Your heart is in your chest." He pops the earbuds in Lexi's ears and places the bell on her chest.

Her little eyes light up. "It sounds like a drum," she excitedly says.

"It sure does. Can I listen to your heart now?"

Again my compliant daughter nods her head, if she really was sick, she'd be squirming and refusing to do as she's told. "Thank you." He pops the earpiece in his ears and looks down at her. "Okay, Lexi, I'm going to pop this on your chest and when I do, I want you to take big deep breaths for me."

"Okay." She does as asked, breathing in and out deeply.

"A few more and then we're done." She keeps breathing and he moves it around her chest and when he's finished, he removes the earpiece and asks her to stick her tongue out. She sticks it out and he nods at her.

Looking up at me, he puts me at ease. "Everything sounds clear. Her temperature is a little high but not worrisome. Her throat is a little red but with rest and fluids, she'll be okay."

"Preston, are you sure?" I question. Seeing him all doctor like makes me reconsider that she wasn't faking after all. Dropping next to her, I press my hand to her forehead and check her temperature again.

He nods and smiles. "Positive. Bed rest and *My Little Pony* is what I'd prescribe."

"*My Little Pony*, really?" I say, rolling my eyes at him.

"Yep," he says, tapping Lexi on the tip of her nose in a loving way that has my ovaries clenching. My hoo-ha sings, "Touch me. Feel me."

Hearing Lexi giggle eases my worries and I watch as Preston fusses over her, seeing him with her makes me all giddy. "...and don't forget, *My Little Pony* and lots of drinks."

"Okay, Doc," Lexi coos.

"You could have prescribed *Outlander* or something."

He looks over to me. "Well, for Mommy, I'd prescribe a date…with me."

"That line ever work before?" I tease.

"Depending on your answer, I'll let you know."

"Ohh, I like him," Mom says from the sofa. "Cress, I'll take Lexi to bed, leave you two alone." Mom winks at me, stands up and holds out her hand to Lexi. Lexi hops up, gives me a kiss, and walks over to Mom.

"It was lovely to meet you, Dr. Knight," Mom says, her voice all dreamy.

"Just Preston is fine."

Lexi turns back to Preston with a quizzical look on her face. "Why are you called Dr. Knight if you is also nameded Preston?"

"My full name is Preston Knight, so people can call me Dr. Knight or Preston."

She's nods in agreement. "Mine is Alexis Avery Bayliss but people just call me Lexi, or Lex. And Mommy sometimes calls me Munchkin. I call Mommy, Mommy but Nanna and Ave called her Cress, or Cressida when she's in trouble."

"Lexi," Mom says with a laugh, "let's get you into bed so you can rest and be better for school on Monday."

"Okay, Nanna."

Lexi takes Mom's hand. "Good night, Preston," Mom says on her way out of the living room.

"Good night, Momma Cress, it was lovely to meet you."

"Momma Cress, I like that," Mom croons. I roll my eyes, this guy is smooth but it's not in a creepy over-the-top way. It's endearing and sweet. He has both Mom and Lex wrapped around his finger. Mom and Lexi walk out of the room and it's now, just Preston, me, and my thumping libido.

We stare at one another, from down the hallway we hear Lexi tell Mom, "I wish he was a real knight and not a doctor knight. A real knight would have a horse and a sword."

At the mention of sword, my eyes drop to his crotch and I imagine what his sword would look like. Breaking the silence, Preston says, "So," my eyes lift back to his, "what do you say?"

"To what?" I play coy.

"A date?"

Staring at him, I make him sweat a little. "I guess I could lower my standards and date a doctor who moonlights as an Uber driver."

He chuckles at my reply. "There is one condition to this date."

"Ohh, yeah and what's that?"

He steps toward me and whispers, "You need to teach me how to horizontal tango at some point during the evening."

"I'm sure if you play your cards right, that can be arranged." Pursing my lips, I try to hold back the smile that's threatening to break free. "When will this date slash teaching lesson happen?"

"I'm free Wednesday night?"

Not wanting to seem too eager, even though given the choice, I'd leave again right now with him. "I'll have to see if Mom ca—"

"Mom's available," Mom yells from down the hallway.

We both laugh.

"Seems we have a date on Wednesday," he says, pulling a card out of the side of his medical bag. Picking up a pen from the coffee table, he scribbles on the back of it. "Here's my card, my cell is on the back. I'll pick you up here at 7 p.m. on Wednesday." He kisses my cheek and picks up his bag. Before he walks out, he gazes at me, my body temperature rising with the intensity of his stare and that déjà vu feeling envelops me again. "Goodnight, Cress."

"Goodnight Preston."

With those parting words, he leaves.

Staring at the living room entrance, I'm all smiles. I love hearing my name pass through his lips…I can't wait to feel those lips on mine and hopefully on Wednesday, I will.

Flopping back onto the sofa, I lean back and grin, I have a date with Dr. Knight.

4 CRESS

The next morning, we have breakfast with Mom and then we head home. All signs of a fever and sickness gone. Once home, I put in a load of laundry and Lexi plays in her room while I continue to tidy up. As I'm putting the vacuum cleaner away, I realize I'm still smiling. Last night with Preston was pretty amazing. Nothing physical has happened between us—yet—but the connection and spark is there. I haven't felt that in a long time, not since Creed. My thoughts are interrupted when from the living room I hear the theme song to *My Little Pony*. "Fuck me," I mumble to myself.

Closing the linen cupboard door, I head out to see my munchkin. Leaning over the back of the sofa, I kiss her forehead and am happy to still feel no temperature. "Hey, Munchkin, it's a bit early for Pony isn't it?"

She shakes her head and looks up at me. "Dr. Knight said it was my medicine."

"I don't think he said that."

She nods again. "Yes, he did. He said prescribe *My Little Pony* and Nanna said prescribe means medicine when she tucked me in."

"Did she now?"

"Yep," she replies as if butter wouldn't melt in her mouth. Shaking my head, I head into the kitchen and turn on my coffee machine. I need caffeine if I'm going to deal with Twilight Sparkle and her pals…for the fifty-millionth time.

With my coffee in hand and a juice box for Lexi, I head back into the living room. Taking a seat next to Lex, I pass her her juice box and grab my phone and Preston's card.

CRESS: *Thank you for last night. Sorry to end it how we did*

Placing my phone next to me, I grab my iPad and scan Facebook and Instagram before I start playing a game. I'm just about to win this level when my phone beeps with a text, startling me and I lose. "Duck me," I mumble to myself, as I swipe into messages and smile when I see it's from Preston.

PRESTON: *Morning, love. It's fine. How's the patient this morning?*
CRESS: *She's good. Currently taking her medicine of* My Little Pony *and washing it down with an apple juice box.*
PRESTON: *That's great. How's Mommy this morning?"*

Missing you is my first thought but I can't tell him that.

CRESS: *Great, I have coffee and a healthy daughter*
CRESS: *Thank you again for checking her over last night*
CRESS: *I really appreciate it*
PRESTON: *It was my pleasure.*
PRESTON: *You can pay be back on Wednesday night **wink wink***
CRESS: *I didn't realize there was a house call fee, how will I ever repay you?*
PRESTON: *I can think of a few ways **wink wink***
CRESS: *Are you proposing sexual favors for your work?*
PRESTON: *If you're offering, I'm not going to say no…what sane man would say no to that? I was just proposing dinner…and maybe a horizontal tango lesson*
CRESS: *Maybe we can compromise*
PRESTON: *I'm open to suggestions*
CRESS: *We can discuss this Wednesday in great detail*
PRESTON: *Is it Wednesday yet?*
CRESS: *Someone's anxious*
PRESTON: *I have a hot date with a sexy as fuck woman who may, or may not, teach me how to horizontal tango…you'd be anxious too*
CRESS: *Meh, but I am looking forward to Wednesday*
PRESTON: *You and me both, love*
CRESS: *Bye, Preston :)*
PRESTON: *Later, gator*
CRESS: *Later, gator? Really?*
PRESTON: *Does later, mater work better?*
PRESTON: *Or see ya later, alligator*
PRESTON: *Or take care, teddy bear*

PRESTON: *Or bye bye, butterfly*
CRESS: *Please stop…I get it, you're a big kid at heart*
PRESTON: *That's not the only thing that's big **wink wink***

My eyes go wide at his response but at the same time, it doesn't surprise me at all. This man is an enigma and for some reason, he wants me. Well, I think he wants me, and I think I want him too.

CRESS: *No one likes a bragger*
PRESTON: *It's not bragging if it's true*
CRESS: *Who says it's true?*
PRESTON: *I do*
CRESS: *You don't count*
PRESTON: *I do too….1, 2… skip a few… 99, 100*
PRESTON: *See, I can count*
CRESS: *I'm going now.*
CRESS: *Bye, Preston :)*
PRESTON: *Goodbye, love*

God, I love it when he calls me love, I think to myself as I read back over our text messages. He really is a big kid, but he's a big kid with a heart of gold. The way be stepped up last night with Lexi was beautiful, and he was great with her.

Throwing my phone onto the coffee table, I sit back and lose myself in *My Little Pony* but my thoughts keep drifting to Preston and our upcoming date. Needing a distraction, I tell Lexi to go get dressed.

We head to the park and I push Lexi on the swings, she's always loved the swings. Out of all the equipment in the park, she always makes a beeline for the swing. We are finishing up an ice cream when my phone rings. I look at the screen and smile when I see it's Ave. "Afternoon, hussy," I tease when I answer.

"Morning," she replies, her voice rough with sleep.

"Sooo…" I prompt my tight-lipped friend, "how was your night?"

"Good," she offers in reply.

"Good, that's all I get…good?"

"Yep. I'm in a taxi on my way home right now." She sighs and then whines, "Cress—"

"I'll be there when you get home," I say without a second thought, Ave has always been there for me, now it's my turn to be there for her. Grabbing Lexi's hand, we head back to my Toyota. Once she's strapped in, we stop at Walmart and I grab the essentials: wine, ice cream, and chocolate.

Forty minutes later, Lexi and I pull up at Ave's apartment, which she shares with her twin, Baylor. I hope she's not home because at the moment, that woman is a selfish bitch and she's horrible to her sister.

Knocking on the door, I don't wait for an answer, I waltz in and notice Ave is still in last night's dress and she looks well-fucked, and on edge. She needs wine and a debrief.

"Lexi, how you doing?" she says, as she hugs my daughter.

"I'm good, Aunty A. I got to sleep at Nanna's last night and Mommy took me to the park and I got an ice cream."

"So I can see. What flavor did you get?"

"Mint chocolate chip."

"Yummo, my fav," Ave says, she licks her fingers and wipes a smudge off Lexi's face. She looks to me and smiles, but it doesn't reach her eyes. She's in Ave-freak-out mode right now. "You wanna watch some Pony while Mom and I chat in the kitchen?"

"Yessssss," Lexi squeals in delight. She races into the living room, pulls out her beanbag, and settles in while Ave switches it on. I head into the kitchen and before I do anything, I pour two glasses of wine. The theme song starts to play and then Ave walks into the kitchen, she smiles when she sees her wine waiting. It's the first genuine smile from her since I arrived.

"Okay, spill," I say, as I hand her her glass of wine.

Taking the wine from me, she takes a huge gulp, followed by another. Wow, she's in mega-freak-out mode. "Okay, Chuggy McChuggerson, slow down there," I tease, taking the glass from her and since I'm a good friend, I top it up.

Looking over to her, I see the tears in her eyes. "Cress, I'm a big fat whore," she cries. Stepping to her I envelop her in a hug. Rubbing her back, I let her cry and get it all out. "I slept with him so many times and it was ducking amazing." I smile that at a time like this, she still doesn't swear. We don't, well we try not to, swear when Lexi is around but she's so engrossed in *My Little Pony* I doubt she'd notice. "It was the best ducking sex of my life. I'm surprised I'm not waddling today. When he was asleep, I snuck out, and now I feel guilty for leaving him like that. I can't even apologize for being such a ducking whore. At least I folded his clothes before I left."

That last line stumps me, so I pull back and look quizzically at her. "You folded his clothes?"

She nods her head. "Yeah, when I slipped my dress back on, I picked his clothes up, folded them, and placed them neatly on the coffee table."

I laugh because only my friend would have a one-night

stand and then clean before leaving. And that, right there, is one of the many many reasons I love her.

"Cress," she whines, "I'm a big fat whore."

"NO!," I shout. Stepping back over to her, I wipe under her eyes with my thumb and glare at her with my mom stare. "You are a sexy single gal, who had a fantabulous night ducking a hot guy."

"But—"

"NO! NO! NO! NO! NO! Avery Evans, look at me." She lifts her gaze to meet mine. "One night of amazing sex does not make you a whore. Did he pay you?"

"No."

"Then by definition you are not a whore, maybe a skank, but definitely not a whore."

"Takes a skank to know a skank."

Just like that, everything is right with the world again. "Stop with the guilt for sneaking out."

"How did you know?" she questions.

"I know all your tics, Ave." I hand her her wine back, and she takes a sip, a small one this time. "Now, listen to me, I'm only going to say this once. You will not call yourself a whore for having fantabulous sex. You will not feel guilty for sneaking out like the harlot, which I'm finally able to say my best friend is. I'm proud, wee skankhopper. We, well you, are going to put last night with the sexy Scottish—"

"Irish."

"You are going to put last night with that sexy Irish doctor into the flick bank and move on."

"I knew you were my best friend for a reason. In half—"

"Three-quarters," I tease.

"Fine, in three-quarters of a glass of wine, you've eased my fears and I feel like me again."

"Happy to be of service." I lean on the countertop and rest my chin on my palm. "Now, I want all the sexy filthy details."

She shakes her head at me. "Nope, last night is firmly locked away in my, what did you call it?"

"Flick bank."

"Yes, flick bank. Last night is safely locked away there. Now, I'm going to have a shower 'cause I smell like sex. You can order food and then we can watch *My Little Pony* with Lexi."

"Can't we watch something else?"

"Do you want to enrage your daughter?"

"Fair point."

Lifting my wine, I take a sip and watch as my best friend heads toward her room to shower. She turns around. "Cress, thanks for being you and calming me down."

"You are most welcome, babe. It's not often I get to rescue you, so it's nice to repay the favor for once…even if you won't spill the sexy schmexy details with your BFF."

"Love you," she calls out as she walks away. Grabbing my phone, I call and order Indian, then I join Lexi in the living room AND I manage to get her to watch the *Scooby Doo* movie with Buffy and her hubby. As we watch them on spooky island, my mind keeps drifting to Preston and I wonder if I will feel like Ave come Thursday morning, a dirty satisfied whore…but without the freak-out part.

5 PRESTON

CRESS AND I HAVE BEEN MESSAGING EACH OTHER NONSTOP since I dropped her home last night. And damn, that woman can take something so sweet and innocent and turn it dirty as fuck. I thought Flynn was crass but 'Crass Cress' takes that crown. Now I'm picturing her in nothing but fuck-me heels and a crown—totally saving that for the spank bank. Hey, I'm a man.

Shaking my head, I move on from that delicious sexy thought and get back to what I was originally thinking about, a fully clothed Cress and our upcoming date. She's witty and fun and the banter over text has been amazing. And as sad as it is to admit, this sexting has been the most fun I've had in a long time. Our dirty chats aren't just sexy as fuck, they are funny, honest, and real.

Just like her.

My mind once again drifts to her and specifically her legs, her killer legs…in sexy fuck-me heels and a crown. "Fuuuuck," I groan, readjusting my hardening cock. I'm hard every time I think of her. And that's seriously messing with my mind, I've spent maybe an hour with this woman and a bit longer texting her but man, do I want that woman. Another shocker, I'm looking forward to Wednesday night. Me? Preston Knight is looking forward to a date. There's a definite spark between us. I know women have that seventh sense shit, but I'm positive she feels this pull too. I noticed the way she looked at me because it's exactly how I was looking at her and guess what, love? I'm more than ready to give you a taste of me and I'm more than ready to have a taste of her.

All of her.

She's not like anyone else I have met or been with. She's the complete package. Personality, check. Strong mind, check. Sassy, fun, and witty; check, check, and check. Gorgeous, big check. Sexy as fuck legs, check. Those legs? Fuck those killer legs are all I can think about. You may think something's wrong with me since I keep referring to her legs whereas most men love tits. Big ones, small ones, fake one. Tits ARE the first thing we notice and don't get me wrong, Cress has great boobs...there are so many sinful things I want to do to them, but it's her legs that have me drooling. I keep thinking about her tango lesson, the horizontal kind, where her legs are wrapped about me. My hands, or tongue, running up and down them...Fuck, I can't wait for my horizontal tango lesson on Wednesday. I'm looking forward to see what she's got in store. There's something about Cressida Bayliss and I cannot wait to find out more.

Flynn called and asked to meet me for drinks at The Fat Fox. I'm happy to oblige and we agree to meet in an hour. I walk in, head straight to the bar, and order myself a scotch. With my drink in hand, I find a table and wait for Flynn to arrive. My eyes flick around the bar and a smile graces my face as I think about Cress and her killer legs. My cock twitches in my pants. *Down, boy, we are in public.* My thoughts are interrupted when Flynn arrives. "Hey," he says, taking the seat across from me. He picks up my drink and slams it back. "Rough night?" I question.

"Amazing night. Rough afternoon." He flags down the waitress, and orders himself a beer and another scotch to replace mine that he just chugged back.

"That's two extremes."

"That's how the last eighteen hours have gone."

"Huh?"

He fills me in on last night—lucky bastard—and then what happened this afternoon: unlucky bastard. "The only reason I knew she was there and that I didn't dream the night up was because she folded my clothes and left them on the coffee table."

"She what?"

"Before she left, she folded my clothes that were left in the living room last night."

"At least she's neat."

"Not what I'm focusing on at the moment." His eyes suddenly brighten. "How did you go last night?" Not wanting to share the details just yet, I nonchalantly shrug my shoulders. "What does that mean?"

"It means I looked after the friend like you requested."

"Aaaaand?" he probes.

"And nothing. We had a drink after you guys left and then I dropped her home."

"Really? You didn't fuck her?" he questions me.

"Nope, my dick stayed in my pants. By the sound of things, you had enough sex for the both of us last night and this morning." Taking a sip of my scotch, I ask, "So what are you going to do?"

"No clue. Did you get the friend's details at all?"

Without thinking I shake my head. "Nope, sorry. I was a gentleman and dropped her home like the knight that my last name is."

From the look on Flynn's face, he knows I'm full of shit but that's the best thing about our friendship, we don't push each other to open up and gossip like girls. He knows that when I'm ready to share, I will. And like always, he'll be there to listen with an open ear and a cold beer.

Flynn is pissed about being fucked and ducked and isn't in the mood to socialize, so he calls it a night. As he walks out, I think about Cress and decide to text her again.

PRESTON: *Hey, love. How's the patient now?*

CRESS: *We tried a new medicine,* Scooby Doo, *she's out cold and no further temperatures*

PRESTON: *You really shouldn't mix medicines but in this instance, I will say it was a good choice.*

CRESS: *Personally, I'd prefer* Outlander *but not sure that's appropriate for a five-year-old…what with all the sex, naked boobs and butts, and whatnot*

PRESTON: *I'd like to see your naked whatnot **wink***

CRESS: *Maybe on Wednesday I could be persuaded*

PRESTON: *Dammit, now I'm thinking about you naked in my bed*

CRESS: *Who said anything about a bed????*

PRESTON: *Dammit, woman, stop*

CRESS: *Stop what? Me being naked, caressing my breasts, water cascading down my shoulders between my thighs making me wet*

PRESTON: *Stop it or I'm driving over there right now*

CRESS: *I wouldn't be opposed to that but…*

PRESTON: *But what???*

CRESS: *But A. I'm not at Mom's. B. You don't know where I live C. I'm not at home and D. I'm not that easy*

PRESTON: *Where are you?*

CRESS: *Not at home*

CRESS: *I'm with Ave…she freaked out after last night*

PRESTON: *I was just with Flynn…he's bummed she ran out*

CRESS: *I think she is too…should we play matchmaker?*

PRESTON: *Hell no…if it's meant to be, it will be*

CRESS: *That's very philosophical of you*

PRESTON: *There's a lot you don't know about me, Cressida Bayliss*

CRESS: *It's Cress…and I can't wait for Wednesday to find out more about the elusive Dr. Preston Knight*

CRESS: *Night, Preston*

PRESTON: *See you soon, raccoon*

PRESTON: *Hang on, that one was corny…Take care, polar bear*

Laughing, I pocket my phone and head home, where I fall into bed and dream sexy things about Cress, me, her legs, and a crown…why is Wednesday so far away?

6   CRESS

Wednesday finally rolls around and to say I'm nervous is an understatement. I can't remember the last time I was like this before a date. I'd love to chat with Ave at the moment, but she's still in a funk about fucking and ducking Flynn and to add to her plate, Bitchy Baylor is at it again. It's mind-boggling that those two are twins; they are total opposites. One's a mega bitch, the other is the most beautiful human being on the planet.

I've just dropped Lexi at school and I'm folding the wash when my phone beeps with a text.

PRESTON: *Can't wait for tonight, love*

There's that love again. I get chills every time I see that in a message, I know I should reply but I'm at a loss for words. This man is doing things to me that I normally wouldn't. For instance, a date. I cannot remember the last time I went on a date. Being a single mom is hard, so apart from the occasional hookup or lapse in judgment when Creed would drop Lexi off, it's just been her and me. Am I ready to allow someone into our bubble? Am I ready to try a relationship? With Preston? The sexting has been fun, something that's totally not me but at the same time, I feel special when he reaches out to me. I'm so confused right now. My phone pings with another text and I realize I've been thinking about Preston for the last ten minutes.

PRESTON: *Cat got your tongue?*

CRESS: *No…just busy*

PRESTON: *Whatcha doing?*

CRESS: *Folding wash. What you doing?*

PRESTON: *Just pulled 3 Lego bricks out of a kid's ass*

CRESS: *No way?*

PRESTON: *Yes way, he wanted to shit bricks for show-and-tell so he shoved 3 up his ass on Tuesday last week, ready for show-and-tell this week*

CRESS: *No shit*

PRESTON: *That's why he came he…hasn't shit in a week and his ass was hurting*

CRESS: *Clearly this kid didn't prep properly, everyone knows you need to prepare for anal*

PRESTON: *Cress, he was 7*

CRESS: *Didn't think of that*

PRESTON: *Sooo, what are you open to?*

CRESS: *I'm open to most things*

CRESS: *But not bestiality…or incest…or clowns*

PRESTON: *Clowns, really? So the circus is out then*

CRESS: *NO CIRCUS OR CLOWNS*

CRESS: *EVER*

CRESS: *PERIOD*

CRESS: *I WILL END YOU IF I SEE A CLOWN OR HIGH-TOP TENT*
PRESTON: *Duly noted, no clowns*
PRESTON: *What specifically are YOU open to? **wink wink***
CRESS: *Anything…and everything else*
PRESTON: *Really?*
CRESS: *Really, really. Now I need to finish this wash and prep for a date tonight*
PRESTON: *Is this date good-looking?*
CRESS: *He's all right*
PRESTON: *Only all right?*
CRESS: *I'll let you know later tonight. Bye, Preston*
PRESTON: *Bye bye, butterfly*

Laughing, I throw my phone onto the coffee table and realize that I was pretty open and crass in our communications just now. "Crass Cress strikes again," I say to myself. Preston doesn't seem to mind, we seem to be on the same wavelengths with most things and the banter has been fun, and sexy AF. He and I get along quite well, considering he's a doctor and I'm a single mom. I can't wait for tonight to see if it was just a heat of the moment thing, or if there is something between us. He's great with Lexi and that there is the kicker. She is my everything and I will not let anyone or anything hurt her. Jinxing myself, my phone rings with *his* ringtone. Knowing that if I don't answer, he will harass me until I do, I pick it up and answer, "Hello."

"Babydoll," Creed says in a tone that grates on my nerves. How I was ever in love with this douche canoe is beyond me.

"What can I do for you?"

"So formal, is that any way to speak to your baby daddy?"

Rolling my eyes, I sigh, thankful he cannot see me right now. "Hi, Creed, how are you? To what do I owe the pleasure of this call?"

"No need to be a bitch," he snarls. "Wanna see the squirt."

"You know you are welcome to see her anytime. Just let me know when."

"Tonight."

Of fucking course he wants to see her tonight.

"We have plans tonight, can we do tomorrow?"

"What plans to do you have?"

"My plans are none of your business. You can see her after school tomorrow?"

"Fine," he huffs. "I'll see you both then, Babydoll."

Before I can reply he hangs up. Throwing my phone back to the table, I fall back onto the sofa and shake my head. Of course the universe will throw Dickwad Dawson at me when I'm about to go on a date that I'm excited about. "Fuck you, universe!" I shout to the empty room. Letting out a frustrated sigh, I stand up and begin folding the clothes again, hoping to distract myself.

I'm putting away the last of the laundry when I have an epiphany, Dawson is a moot point. He has nothing to do with my date tonight, I will deal with him tomorrow. Tonight, I'm going to go out with Preston, have a fantabulous time and teach him to tango; vertically AND maybe, horizontally too.

With a renewed excitement, I head into my bathroom and begin preparing for tonight. Stripping off, I fill the sink, grab my razor and shave—everywhere. Once I'm smooth as a baby's butt all over, I run myself a bath. A soak in the tub is just what I need to relax and mentally prepare for tonight. Drizzling in my fav soak, I climb in, moaning as I slide down. The water is a little hot but it eases my muscles and is just what I need right now. Leaning back, I close my eyes and think about Preston. My clit begins to pulse as I picture him; muscular arms, chiseled jaw, gorgeous smile, eyes that bore deep into my soul. Sliding my hand down my body, I press on my throbbing clit and moan. Lifting my leg up, I rest it over the edge of the tub and slip my finger between my folds and push it inside. With my other hand, I massage and squeeze my breast. Pinching my nipple between my thumb and forefinger. His name slips through my lips, "Preston," as my pleasure builds. Slipping a second finger in, I speed up my thrusts, squeezing my breasts harder. Closing my eyes, I shout, "Preston!" as I explode around my fingers. The fiercest self-induced orgasm I've ever had tears through my body, leaving me sated and relaxed.

Opening my eyes, I pull my leg back into the tub and slide down, submerging myself under the water. Blowing out the air in my lungs, à la Julie Roberts in *Pretty Woman*. Breaking the surface, I lean back and sigh. "Fuck me," I mumble as I close my eyes and wait for my heart rate to return to normal. Once I'm me again, I climb out, hop into the shower so I can wash my hair since I dunked myself. If I don't, I'll end up with a frizzy mop, and that's the last thing I want for tonight.

Climbing out of the shower, I dry off and slip on my robe. Plugging in my hair dryer, I dry my hair and then straighten it. I can never blow-dry my hair like the hairdresser does, it always ends up a frizzy mess—thank God for straighteners—at least I can do that. Once my hair is silky smooth, I grab some sexy lingerie and redress.

Looking at the time, I see I have just enough time to grab a coffee before I head to school to pick Lexi up. Pulling on my jeans and a tank top, I grab my keys, slip into my flip-flops, and head out the door.

Twenty minutes later, I'm at school waiting for Lexi to get out. The bell rings and all hell breaks loose. There are kids and parents everywhere. Like a heat-seeking missile, my eyes land on Lexi and when she sees me she waves and races toward me. Dropping to my knees, I open my arms wide. "Hey, Munchkin."

"Hi, Mommy," she replies as I envelop her in a hug.

"You give the best hugs," I tell her, as I place a kiss on the tip of her nose.

"I know," she says with a grin. "I can't wait to sleep at Nanna's tonight."

"She can't wait for you to either."

"Will you be staying with us, like on the weekend?"

"Not tonight, sweetie, I don't want to disturb you since it's a school night."

She nods. "That's a goodly thing. You're a goodly mommy." *Damn, Baylor*, I think to myself hearing Lexi use goodly. Yes, it's a real word but it so does not fit this context. "Are we going to Nanna's now?"

"We can if you want, OR we can swing by the park?"

"Park then home then Nanna's. That's such a goodly idea, Mommy." I shake my head at the use of goodly, again.

"Okay, let's go." She places her hand in mine and we head to the car.

Twenty minutes later, we are at the park and as usual, Lexi makes a beeline for the swings. My phone beeps with a text and I smile when I pull it out.

PRESTON: *T-minus 3 hours and 12 minutes 'til my tango lesson*

A smile graces my face as I read his message. It's nice to know he's as excited as I am for tonight.

CRESS: *Remind me again what's happening in T-minus 3 hours and 11 minutes*
PRESTON: *The best night of your life will commence*
CRESS: *That's a big call to make, Dr. Knight. You better bring your 'A' game stud*
PRESTON: *Ohh, I plan to, love, AND I'm hoping to hit a home run…multiple times*
PRESTON: *See you soon you sexy, raccoon*
PRESTON: *That's totally not really sexy but you are so there's that. Laters, love*
CRESS: *Later, mater **blowing kiss emoji***

Sliding my phone back into my pocket, I watch Lexi on the swings. My mind drifts to tonight and suddenly, I'm nervous. I think I really like this guy…I can totally see myself falling for Dr. Knight.

7 PRESTON

AFTER TEXTING CRESS ABOUT TONIGHT, I START TO WONDER IF I'm coming on too strong, but her replies seem to indicate I'm not, so I guess I will keep going how I am. As I climb into the shower to get ready for tonight, I shake my head. This woman is turning me into a total girl. I don't think I've ever been this excited before a date, but then again, I have never met a woman as vivacious, sexy, and intriguing as Cress Bayliss.

Stepping under the spray, the hot water hits my shoulders. Closing my eyes, I start to think about our texting/sexting over the last few days. Images of her in the shower with me run through my mind.

Water cascading down her body.

Her nipples erect, a droplet of water waiting to be licked.

The water sliding between her thighs.

Her eyes full of desire.

Her plump lips, moist and waiting to be kissed.

My cock hardens. Gripping it tightly in my fist, I picture Cress. Stopping mid-stroke, I realize I want it to be her doing this. Shocking myself, I turn the tap to cold and let go of my cock. Taking a page from Flynn, I join the blue balls club and decide to wait for tonight. Cress doing this will be so much better than my hand. Thinking of her has my cock coming to life again, so I think of saggy granny tits and it instantly deflates.

Now that my dick is under control, I soap up and wash myself, avoiding my cock because if I touch it, I will grip it and jerk it. But I want more than anything for Cress to have that pleasure later this evening. So I refrain.

Short-term pain, long-term gain.

Stepping out, I wrap my towel around my waist and walk over to the dresser. Styling my hair, I stare at my reflection. I look different, I realize my eyes are brighter than usual…I think it's to do with Cress. She's bringing me to life, prior to meeting her I was just existing. I wasn't living, she makes me want to live life…and I hope she wants to do it with me.

Stepping into my room, I get dressed. Black slacks, deep purple dress shirt with the sleeves rolled to my elbow; smart but casual. As I slip my shoes on, I start to wonder what Cress will wear tonight. Whatever she wears, I know she is going to be sexy as fuck.

Looking at the clock on my bedside table, I realize it's time to go. I'm suddenly nervous but at the same time, super excited. Grabbing my wallet and keys, I head into the garage. Pushing the button on the wall, the garage door opens. I climb into my car and start the engine, "Closer" by Nine Inch Nails begins to play. This song is sexy and dirty…*a good sign for tonight*, I think to myself as I back out of the driveway.

On the drive over to pick Cress up, I stop and grab a bunch of flowers. Not knowing what her favorite are, I grab a bouquet of sunflowers, which happens to be my mom's favorite flower. With my flowers in hand, I get back on the road and my nerves settle; that is until I open the door at her mom's. My mouth drops open at the vision before me. Cress is wearing a blood red halter dress that hugs her body in the sexiest possible way. There's a split up the side accentuating her legs, her hair is straighter than straight, and her lips are stained red to match her dress. "Fuck me, you are a vision, Cressida Bayliss."

"Cress," she murmurs, as her cheeks darken. Her eyes roam over my body and my cock appreciates the eye fucking. We silently stare at one another, the air around us thick with desire, want, and need. The moment is broken when Lexi steps beside her mom. "Hey, Dr. Preston."

"Hey, Munchkin, how you feeling now?"

"All better."

"That's great to hear."

"I took my Pony medicine, just like you said."

"Excellent," I say, offering my hand in a high five which she excitedly hits. I shake my hand, pretending it hurts. "Wow, that's a strong high five you have there."

"It's cause I eat all my veggies."

"Did you eat them all up tonight?"

"Yes…even the yucky Brussels sprouts."

I make a face. "I don't like them either." Suddenly I remember the flowers and the little something that I have for Lexi. "Give me a sec," I tell them and race to my car and grab the gifts. Walking back up the path, I hand the flowers to Cress. "These are for you," I say, pressing a kiss to her cheek.

"Thank you," she murmurs, as I drop back down and hand Lexi her gift.

She snatches the gift bag from my hand and pulls out the *My Little Pony: Friendship is Magic* DVD; her eyes light up. "My very own Pony DVD. Thank you, Dr. Preston, thank you." She throws her little arms around my neck and hugs me.

"You are most welcome, Princess."

Looking up, I see Cress holding the flowers in one hand and her other over her heart with an adorable look on her face. Winking at her, her cheeks darken. "Let me pop these in some water and then we can go."

"I can do that," her mom says from behind her.

"Evening, Momma Cress."

"Evening, Preston," she says, taking the flowers from Cress. She winks at her daughter. "You two have fun tonight."

"Mom," Cress scoffs, as she turns around to get her things. My eyes watch as she walks away and her dress from the back is just as stunning.

Momma Cress steps over to me and stares intently at me. "You hurt my baby girl and I'll hurt you. These two girls are all I have left, and I will not let anyone hurt them again. You got me?"

Nodding my head, I confirm, "Yes, ma'am—"

"Don't call me ma'am," she interrupts.

"Yes, Momma Cress. I don't plan on hurting her, or Lexi, or you. Scout's honor." I hold up three fingers and smile.

"Good." Cress walks back toward us, her shoes echoing on the floorboard. "Now you two kids have a great night," she says to Cress, kissing her on the cheek before Cress drops down and hugs Lexi goodbye.

"Be a good girl for Nanna and I will see you in the afternoon after school."

"Nite nite, Mommy." Lexi pulls away and cups her mom's cheek in her hand. Cress stands up and steps beside me. "Bye, Dr. Preston." Lexi says, offering me her fist for a fist bump.

"Bye, Lexi girl," I reply, bumping my fist with hers.

Lexi and Momma Cress head inside and close the door. Looking to Cress, I smile. "Shall we?"

"We shall," she says and links her arm with mine as we walk down the path to my car for our date, one of many... I hope.

8   CRESS

When Preston handed me the flowers, my heart rate sped up at the thoughtfulness of his gift. When he handed Lexi a gift as well, my whole body thrummed with pleasure and my heart soared, especially when I saw what it was. A sob built in the back of my throat as I watched Preston with the most important person in my life, the scene before me was so beautiful. The connection he has with Lexi is strong already. I can tell that if this goes off the rails between us, she too will be heartbroken. Then Mom arrives and even she is smitten with him. Damn, we will all be gutted if this turns to shit. Maybe I need to back off and keep them apart until I know what this is between us.

Mom takes the flowers from me when I offer to pop them in water, but I'm thankful, as I don't really want to leave her alone with Preston, who knows what would occur. As I rejoin them, I bite the inside of my cheek to hold back my laugh when Mom scolds him for calling her ma'am.

We say our goodbyes, with a fist bump for Preston and Lexi—it totally melts my heart seeing that—and then he escorts me to his car. With each step we take down the path, my nerves ramp up. My eyes land on his car and I smile. "Your car is pretty sexy, Dr. Knight."

"As are you, Ms. Bayliss." He reaches around me and opens my door.

"Thank you, Sir."

"No thank you, Love. Thank you for allowing me to wine and dine you tonight."

"You just want the promised horizontal tango lesson."

"That's just an added bonus." He pauses and looks at me, his gaze heating my skin, and again that déjà vu feeling washes over me. "Cress, tonight is just the beginning of something beautiful." With those words, he closes my door. *Holy shit*, we haven't even left the house yet and I'm already swooning for this man.

He pulls into a parking garage and we climb out. My eyes rake over his car and I shake my head, this is one sexy car...for a sexy as hell man. "Shall we?" he says, offering me his elbow.

"We shall."

Linking my arm through his, we make our way to the elevator and take it down to the street level. We step out and cross the road. My eyes light up when I see we are walking toward, Las Tapas. It's a mom-and-pop run Spanish restaurant. "Ohh, I love this place."

"Me too, they make the best—"

"–paella," we say together and laugh.

Things are so easy with Preston, I can definitely see myself falling for this man and that scares me. I haven't felt like this with anyone since Creed, and we all know how that turned out.

We step inside and while we wait to be seated, we look at one another, and again that déjà vu feeling appears. "Have we met before?" I ask.

Preston shakes his head. "I don't think so, but occasionally when I gaze at you I get this feeling like we have."

Nodding my head, I smile. "It's so weird."

"Well, either way, I'm glad I get to know you now," he says, just as the hostess arrives and escorts us to our table.

Las Tapas is your typical Spanish restaurant. Gorgeous Spanish inspired artwork lines the walls, crystal chandeliers hang from the ceiling. There's custom-made bar tops with handmade Spanish tiles and natural wood. Wine racks full of wine line the walls and large windows overlook the outdoor dining area. Each table is set with candles, making it intimate and perfect for our first date, by creating the perfect romantic dining experience.

Preston pulls out my chair and pushes it in. The heat from his body sets mine ablaze, he didn't even touch me and I'm already turned on, panting and wanting more. Thankfully the waitress arrives and hands us our menus.

"Buena noches, what can I get you to drink?"

"Can I grab a glass of Tempranillo, please?"

"Make it a bottle," Preston says.

"Por supuesto," the waitress replies, turning away from us, she makes her way back to the bar, leaving Preston and me alone for the first time since we sat down.

We stare at each other across the table. I lick my bottom lip and gently bite, my go-to movement when I'm nervously excited. This man does things to me, even without laying a hand on me. I notice his eyes locked on my lips, then he looks into my eyes. His stare penetrates deep into my soul. My body thrums with desire. I swallow deeply. Neither of us has spoken but so much has been said with our eyes.

I want you.

I desire you.

I need you.

The waitress returns with the wine but we keep staring at each other. She silently opens the bottle and fills our glasses. She turns and as she walks away, I hear her silently whisper, "That was caliente."

We both laugh.

Picking up his glass, he raises it in a toast, "To the beginning of something amazing."

"I'll drink to that."

Tapping my glass against his, I take a sip and moan in delight. "Ohh wow, that's a good vintage." Looking up, I see Preston staring at me open-mouthed. "What? Do I have something on my face?"

He shakes his head, "No, that sound you just made had my mind going to a dirty sexy place…with you."

"Do tell, Dr. Knight," I playfully tease, resting my elbows on the table and my chin in my palm, blinking rapidly at him. When I stop with the blinking, I realize that probably looks like I'm having a fit rather than the sexy siren I was going for.

He leans forward, "Well…" But before he can tell me all the dirty sexy things, the waitress arrives.

"Are you ready to order?"

"The paella," we both say at the same time.

"el amor está floreciendo," the waitress says with a smile, before turning around and leaving us alone again.

"What did she just say?" I ask, my voice laced with confusion and intrigue.

"Beats me," Preston shrugs. "But she seems pretty happy right now, so I'm guessing it was something good."

"It was very good," the lady at the table next to us says.

We both turn our heads to see an elderly couple at the table.

"What did she say?" Preston asks her.

"Love is blossoming," her husband says, He takes his wife's hand in his and brings it to his lips and kisses her knuckles. She smiles adoringly at him, love radiates between the two of them. "Lucia and I had paella on our first date sixty-five years ago. Love is the food of life. Paella is life therefore paella is the food of life and love. And Lucia is my life and love. "

"That is beautiful. I wish you many more years of love and paella."

"Salud," he says, raising his wine glass toward us.

Preston and I raise ours in return and both say, "Salud." We gaze at one another, our eyes are locked on each other, as we sip the wine.

We are both quiet, processing the man's words.

Lucia and her husband stand up and leave. I watch as they walk away, he gently rests his hand on her lower back; that is unbridled true love. Looking to Preston, I smile. "Wow, can you imagine being with someone for that long?"

"I'll let you know in sixty-five years." Preston replies, the look in his eye is carnal.

Lifting my wine to my lips, I take a sip and stare at Preston over the rim of the glass. This man continues to amaze me, I keep thinking I'm going to wake up because sexy doctors don't want me. I'm a nobody; therefore this must be a dream. A fucking good dream but it must be a dream nonetheless. Preston squeezes my arm, snapping my attention back to the present and the realization that this is in fact real life.

"You drifted off there, where did you go just now?"

"Nowhere in particular. Just thinking that this must be a dream because I'm on a date with a sexy doctor in an amazing restaurant. Drinking amazing wine about to dine on a fantabulous paella. Things like this don't happen to me. Ever. Therefore this must be a dream."

"You think I'm sexy?"

"That's what you took from what I just said?"

"I took the important parts. I'm sexy and fantabulous paella."

"You are really something, Dr. Knight."

"A good something?"

"I haven't made my mind up yet," I pause for emphasis, "but if tonight keeps proceeding like this, you will definitely be getting that tango lesson before the night is over."

9 PRESTON

Fuck me, this woman is something else. I have never been around a woman like her before. She's sexy as fuck. Vivacious. Flirtatious. Funny. Down-to-Earth. She is the complete package.

Our date is going smoothly. The paella is delicious, both of us moaning in delight with each mouthful. After dinner, we finish off the wine and continue to get to know one another. "…I'm pretty sure I scared Ave off of ever having kids after I nearly crushed her hand when I was in labor."

"You are amazing," I honestly tell her.

"How so?"

"You're raising your daughter alone."

"I'm not alone, I have Ave and Mom."

"No, they help occasionally. *You* are doing all the hard work yourself AND you substitute teach if needed."

"It's nothing compared to what you do."

"Don't sell yourself short, Cress. I think you're

amazing and that's all there is to it. Now, would you like to dance with me?"

She looks over her shoulder and sees a few other couples dancing, that's one of the things I love about this place. People don't care, they just do what feels right, and right now, I want to dance with this woman. Her face lights up. "I'd love to."

Standing up, I step over to her and offer my hand. She places hers in mine and like each time we touch, there's a spark that jolts through me. Spinning her around, I pull her in close to me. One hand sits on her lower back, the other holds her hand between us. She rests her head on my shoulder and we sway to the music. Our bodies becoming one. Taking a deep breath, I breathe in. Her smell envelops me. "I love your scent," I whisper into her hair, breathing everything about her in again. "I could get high breathing you in."

I feel her smile against me. "I've worn this since forever," she quietly says as we continue to dance.

"What is it?"

She lifts her head and gazes into my eyes. "True Love by Elizabeth Arden."

If that isn't a sign of what's to happen between us, I don't know what is. Between her perfume name, the kind words from the waitress, and the love story between Lucia and her husband, we are surrounded by all things love tonight. I can see myself falling for Cressida Bayliss.

Cress rests her head back on my shoulder, her body molding into mine once again. She turns her head and begins to kiss and nuzzle where my neck and shoulder meet. My hand slides down her back and I cup her ass, her perfect taut ass, in my palm. She reaches down and lifts my hand from her ass, placing it back on her lower back. Making a quiet tsking sound as she lets go.

Sliding my hand back down, I squeeze her ass this time. She lifts her head and stares at me. It's the perfect moment for our first kiss. Closing my eyes, I begin to lean forward when she spins away. I realize the music has changed, to a much faster song. She holds my hand and spins in and out in sync with the music. She spins back in, this time her back to my front. She swivels her hips, which has my cock wanting to dance too. There's no hiding what she's doing to my body right now. She glances at me over her shoulder and winks. *Minx*, I think to myself as she spins out again. This time when she spins back in, she slides her hands seductively up and down my chest. She grabs my hands. "Let's dance," she huskily says. The tone of her voice heads straight to my dick and it hardens further between us. I'm frozen, I stare at the sex bomb before me. "Let's tango," she says, as she takes my hands in hers and we begin to tango.

I've always thought this was a sexy dance, but to be involved in said dance, it's even sexier than I imagined. Cress is amazing. Her body flows with the music, pressing seductively into mine and surprising me, I keep up with her. Probably because having her body pressed against mine is the most amazing feeling in the world.

As the song comes to an end, she spins back into me, wrapping my hands around her stomach. She leans her head back and stares at me over her shoulder. We are both breathing heavily. The minx, once again, swivels her hips against my cock. Not letting her win, I press it into her ass. She slides a hand between us and grips my hip, squeezing tight and rubbing her ass in circles on my cock. There's no hiding my desire for her.

"Cress," I warn, but there's no way in hell that's going to stop what she's doing. Right at this moment, I wish we were at home naked doing this.

"What?" she innocently says.

Shaking my head, I surprise her when I spin her out and pull her back in. Sliding my hands into her hair, I pull her to me, and slam my lips against hers. She slides her hands around my shoulders and pulls me closer. Deepening our kiss. As first kisses go, this one takes the cake. Our tongues bump in their own seductive dance. Breaking the kiss, she pulls back and stares at me. We are both panting, the kiss leaving each of us breathless. Ever so slowly, I trace down her spine and place my hand on her ass, gently squeezing. Her lips lift into a smile that lights up her face. She rests her head back onto my shoulder and we lose ourselves to the music, once again slow dancing.

The song ends, we pull apart, staring at one another. Cupping her cheek in my palm, I run my thumb along her jawbone before I lean in and press my lips against hers again. Pulling back, I rest my forehead against hers. "You have the lips of an angel, Cress. Where have you been?"

"Raising my little girl and waiting for you," she whispers. She takes a step back. "Now, take me home, Preston, so I can give you that naked tango lesson I promised."

10 CRESS

As first dates go, this is the best one ever in the history of first dates. Well, for me that's the case and I really hope it is for him too. Preston is the whole package: hot, fun, caring, charismatic, hot—yes I know I said hot twice but hello, he looks like Channing-freaking-Tatum's brother, that deserves two hots. Dancing just now was the most fun I've had in a long time. I cannot remember the last time I danced like this. Come to think about it, it would have been the night Lexi was conceived. Creed took me out to this Latin club and we danced the night away. Shaking my head, I don't want to be thinking of *him* right now. Tonight is all about Preston and me, and possibly the start of something amazing. I'm not sure I'm ready for a relationship but if anyone can sway that decision, it will be Preston Knight.

Lacing my fingers with Preston's we exit the restaurant after he settles the bill. I offered to pay half but ever the gentleman, he wouldn't hear of it. We walk toward his car in the parking garage; the only sound the echoing of my heels clicking on the cement floor. As we approach it, I whistle, "This seriously is a sexy car." I stop and appreciate the machine before me. I don't know shit about cars but I do know, this one is hot.

"I've seen sexier things."

Looking to him, my face is etched with confusion because this is the sexiest car around. "What else could possibly be sexier than this?" I ask, flicking my hand up and down his car.

He steps behind me, I can feel his breath on my skin. "You," he huskily answers, as he slides his hand around my waist, pulling me into him. My head drops back to his shoulder, elongating my throat. He darts his tongue out and licks up my neck, my skin breaks out in goosebumps, and I moan. My hips rub against his crotch, garnering a low growl from him. He cups my cheek, turns my head toward him, and kisses me. This kiss takes my breath away. If his other hand wasn't on my hip holding me up, I'd be a puddle on the floor.

Our tongues dance and caress one another, spinning to face him, I deepen the kiss. Pressing my chest to his. "Take me home, Preston," I whisper against his lips.

Without saying a word, he unlocks the car and opens my door for me. Climbing in, I watch him walk around the hood. His eyes steadfastly locked on mine. He climbs in, starts the car, and speeds toward his place.

We pull into his driveway and the door to the garage automatically opens, he parks and turns the car off. He must sense me watching him because he turns to look at me. My breathing quickens and nerves wrack through me at the intensity of his gaze.

"Cress," he whispers. Reaching over he brushes a

tendril of hair behind my ear and cups my cheek in his palm.

"Pres," I whisper back, leaning into his palm.

He pulls my head toward him and he presses his lips to mine. Cupping his cheeks in my palms I hungrily kiss him back. The temperature in the car rises rapidly. Breaking the connections between us, I whisper, "Take me inside, Pres, I owe you a horizontal tango lesson and I have a feeling you will be the best student ever."

"A's all round for this boy."

"I was hoping for big O's," I playfully tease.

"I'm sure that can be arranged. Inside now, Ms. Bayliss, I'm ready for my lesson."

We climb out and head inside. Preston's place is gorgeous. Large open plan living, dining, and kitchen; which looks like it leads to an outdoor entertainment area. Chrome and black accents, it's very stylish and sophisticated. Exactly how I pictured his place. Noticing a kick-ass stereo system, I head over to it and connect up my Spotify account. I bring up a dance playlist and when I see the perfect song, I hit play. "Closer" by Nine Inch Nails begins to play. My hips move to the beat of the music. Turning around I see Preston staring intently at me, a grin etched on his face.

"This is fate, Cress."

"How so?"

"This song was playing in my car earlier this evening."

"That is the very definition of fate. Now, Dr. Knight, where would you like your lesson?"

"Come with me."

He turns around and walks down the hallway and into the master bedroom. He flicks on the lights, presses a button on the remote, which was sitting on the dresser, and the music from the living room filters into the room. Leaning against the doorframe I watch as he walks over to a chair in the corner. Untucking his shirt from his pants, he takes a seat. Leaning back, he undoes the top two buttons on his shirt, before resting his hands on the arm of the chair. He is the epitome of an alpha male right now. Sexy. Powerful. In charge. The alphaness oozing from him. Seeing him like this sets my body ablaze. I now know how Ana felt in *Fifty Shades* when Christian would watch her; I've never felt sexier than I do right now.

"The floor is yours," he says, gesturing to the space in front of him.

Pushing off the doorframe, my hips sway to the beat of the music. Running my hands up my neck and into my hair, I flick through the strands. Stretching my hands above my head. My eyes are locked on Preston as I slide my hands seductively up and down my sides. With my fingertip, I trace along my cleavage, between the valley of my breasts, down my stomach. Gripping the hem, I lift it up slightly, and shake the material side to side. His eyes are locked on my movements. Stepping over to him, I beckon him forward with my finger.

Preston slides to the edge of the chair, spreading his legs wide for me to stand in front of him. My hips continue to swing to the music. Reaching out, I undo the buttons on Preston's shirt. Tracing my finger up his chest, I circle his nipple. Stepping back, I turn round and look at him over my shoulder. Squatting down, I continue to look at him over my shoulder, standing up I bend forward at the hips, and shimmy my ass in his face. Snapping back into an upright position, I turn to face him again.

His eyes are full of desire and they watch my every

movement. Stepping back, I stare down at him. "Up," I demand.

He stands before me and I slide my hands across his shoulders, dragging his dress shirt down his arms. The material drops to the floor, he's standing before me in nothing but his dress pants. Both of us panting. The song changes to "Cheap Thrills" by Sia. Pushing off his chest, I spin around in circles. Flicking my hips to the beat of the music. Preston steps behind me. He rests his palms on my hips, sliding them down to grip the hem of my dress, and begins to lift it up. "Ah uh," I say. Stepping away, I turn to face him. With my eyes locked on his, I brush my hair over my left shoulder and undo the bow at my neck, sliding my hands around my neck. Letting go of the strap, the material falls to my feet. Leaving me in my black strapless bra and matching panties.

Pushing him back, he falls into the chair. Resting my hands on the arm, I stare at him before pressing myself forward. My body hovering an inch in front of him, I can feel his breath on my chest. Standing up, I brush my chest against his face. A growl erupts from him. With a grin on my face, I step to the center of the room. Turning to face him, I call him forward with my finger. He stands up and prowls over to me. The look on his face sets my body on fire. He stops in front of me. Without saying a word, I undo his belt, pop the button, lower his fly, and push his pants down. We are now both in our underwear. Placing my hand on his lower back, I pull him into me. Taking his hand in mine, I place it on my hip. He grips my other hand and brings it between us.

With our gaze locked on one another we sway side to side. Our movements are not in sync with the music but the moment is pure perfection. He spins me out and back in again, just like we did at the restaurant. He repeats the spin and this time, I end up with my back to his front.

He hugs me to him, nuzzling my neck. "Cress, you are the sexiest woman I have ever met." I moan when he sucks my neck. Dropping my head back onto his shoulder. He finds the front clasp of my bra and flicks it open, my breasts spill free. He cups them in his palms as I swivel my hips on his groin. His cock hardening the more I press against him.

The song comes to an end, and I stay wrapped in his arms. My back to his front. Looking over my shoulder, we stare intently at one another, our chests rapidly rising with each breath we take. He lowers his head and presses his lips to mine, my eyes close and I give myself over to the kiss. He wraps his arms tighter around me, one hand cupping my boob and squeezing. The other slides down my stomach, where he cups my pussy over my panties. I moan. Breaking the kiss, I open my eyes and stare into his. My hips gently rock side to side, his cock pressing into the crack of my ass, the material of our underwear the only barrier.

We are both breathing heavily, the air around us electrified with desire, want, need, and hunger.

Preston slides his other hand down my side, gripping my hips, he tears my panties off before quickly removing his briefs. He presses me into his freed erection. The head of his cock pushing against my ass, a guttural moan breaks free. I've never been as turned on as I am right now. Sliding my hand around his neck, I run my fingers into his hair and gently tug. Our hips still circling and pressing into each other. Lowering my hand, I slide it between us and grip his cock in my palm. Squeezing.

"Cress," he groans.

Spinning around to face him, I lick my bottom lip, with my eyes locked on his, I begin to drop to my knees. He grabs me by the shoulders and pulls me back up into a standing position. He grips my ass and lifts me up, on instinct I wrap my legs around his waist and drape my arms over his shoulders. His thick shaft pressing into my stomach as our mouths crash together in a frenzied kiss. Tightening my arms around his neck, I press myself into him. You cannot tell where I end and he begins.

He sits on the end of the bed with me straddling him. Lifting myself up, I circle myself around the tip of his cock. I begin to lower myself down when he says, "Condom." Standing up, with me still in his arms, he walks around the side of the bed and sits near the head. He reaches into the side table drawer and grabs one. Shuffling back, I take the foil packet from him and tear it open with my teeth. Quickly I sheath his cock and then, once again, I lift up and circle the tip before I sink myself onto him. We both moan in delight as I fully seat myself on him. With our eyes locked on one another, I slowly begin to move my hips in circles. Pushing Preston back, he falls to the bed and I follow. He slides his hands into my hair and pulls my lips to his. Closing my eyes, I focus solely on the feel of his lips on mine, and his cock sliding in and out of me.

"Prestoooon," I mewl, as an intense orgasm detonates out of nowhere.

My walls clench around him while my body tingles from head to toe as pleasure courses throughout my body. My release sets Preston off, his body stiffens beneath me. He groans and grunts as he releases in the condom.

Falling off, I lie next to him panting. Staring at the ceiling and catching my breath. Turning my head to the side, I see Preston looking at me. "Hi," I murmur.

"Hi," he says back, leaning over to me and pressing his lips to mine. "That was the best dance lesson of my life. I think I want to sign up for more."

"I'll have to check my schedule but I'm sure I can fit you in. You are, by far, my best student."

"I better be your only student."

Nodding my head, I smile. "This is a one student only school."

"Good," he says before pressing his lips to mine again. I shudder at the intensity of this kiss; he pulls me into his side and we cuddle. Closing my eyes, I drift off to sleep completely sated and totally falling for Dr. Knight.

11 PRESTON

Opening my eyes, I have a smile on my face. I had the best dream last night, then a soft little snore from beside me garners my attention. Turning my head, I smile when I realize my dream was in fact reality from last night. Cress and I did the tango, both horizontally and vertically, and we did it both clothed and unclothed. My cock clearly remembers because he is proudly standing to attention, hoping for a replay of last night.

Reaching over, I brush a tendril of blonde hair off her forehead, gently grazing her skin as I do. This causes Cress to open her eyes. When she notices me staring at her, she smiles. It lights up her face, the blue of her eyes intensifying as she wakes up.

"Morning, Dr. Knight."

"Morning, Ms. Bayliss."

We stare at one another. She leans toward me, the sheet slipping down, exposing her tits to me. I get the sudden urge to lean forward and suck and bite them. That thought is thwarted when Cress climbs over and straddles my waist. She stares down at me and we silently gaze at one another, the temperature in the room rising by the second. She leans down and places her hands on either side of my head, her eyes boring deep into my soul. Lowering her head, she presses her lips to mine. Opening my mouth, she slides her tongue in. My hands grip her hips, when she begins grinding herself on me. Smearing her arousal on my stomach. She takes my lip between her teeth and gently bites. Letting my lip go, she kisses along my jawline to my ear. She's breathing heavily, much like I am. My heart races with each nip of her teeth on my skin. When she bites my earlobe and sucks it, I groan at the sensation. Pain and pleasure mixing together. I'm not normally into the pain/pleasure side of intimacy but with Cress, I'm willing to try anything; and everything.

Shimmying down, she stops when my rock-hard cock hits her ass. She licks and nibbles her way down my neck and across my collarbone. Sucking and biting my nipple. "Fuuuuck," I moan, increasing my grip on her hips. I want nothing more than to flip her over and fuck her but at the same time, I want to see where this will lead.

Sitting up, she stares down at me and traces the path her tongue just took with her fingertip. My skin is buzzing and burning for this woman. She circles my nipple before twisting and squeezing. I hiss at the sensation, my cock twitches against her ass. Her lips lift in a smirk as her fingertip traces over my abs. I'm not ripped but I am in shape and right now, I'm thankful for the countless hours I've spent in the gym.

She lifts to her knees and I inwardly smile at what's to come next, much to my dismay, she slides her wet pussy over my shaft and straddles my thighs. "Cress," I plead.

The little minx winks at me and leans forward. Her tongue circles my navel before she licks down toward my crotch. She purrs as she licks over the spot where she was grinding herself earlier. *I really want to taste her*, I think to myself as I lift to my elbows and watch her. We stare at one another as her tongue continues south, down to my cock. It's harder than it's ever been before, I cannot wait to see her lips around my shaft. She licks around the base, licking as if it's a melting ice cream on a hot summer's day. She licks up the side, and then back down. I growl because I want my cock in her mouth. She grips my shaft and begins to pump as she sucks one of my balls into her mouth. Humming around me, the sensation is amazing. I've never felt anything like it before.

"Cress," I pant, as I grip her head and pull her mouth off me. "If you don't suck my cock right now, I will not be held accountable for what I do to your mouth."

"Patience, Dr. Knight. Patience," she teases, as she sucks my ball into her mouth, while continuing to pump my shaft up and down with her hand. My ball pops out of her mouth and she licks around the base again, her tongue going higher and higher each time.

She lifts her head and stops. She stares at me, her tongue darts out and flicks over the head of my cock. It's throbbing. I don't know how much longer I can hold back. She winks at me and, finally, covers my cock with her mouth. It's wet. It's warm. It's fucking heaven. Hollowing her cheeks, she sucks my cock into her mouth. The head hits the back of her throat before she pulls out again. Repeating the process over and over until she opens her throat and takes all of my cock into her mouth and down her throat. This is the best blowjob in the history of blowjobs.

She cups my balls and continues to suck on my shaft. Our eyes locked on one another as she blows my mind with her blowjob skills. My balls tighten and then I come. I come like I've never come before. Cress sucks and swallows every last drop. When my cock pops out of her mouth, she wipes the corner of her lips. She leans down and ever so lightly brushes her breasts against my skin. Placing a quick kiss on my lips, she hops off the bed and walks to my en suite. I take the time to appreciate her gloriously naked ass and legs, they are perfect in every way. This ass man is very happy.

She grips the doorframe and looks at me over her shoulder, "I'll have a coffee, black, one sugar, please." She steps into the bathroom and closes the door behind her.

Shaking my head, I climb out of bed and pull on my navy lounge pants and head into the kitchen to get my girl coffee. Yes, I referred to her as my girl, I'm man enough to admit that I am falling for this woman. Grabbing out the coffee grounds, I fill the coffee maker and turn it on. When the coffee is brewed, I make two coffees —one black with one sugar and the other, with hazelnut creamer. I've just finished making them when Cress steps into the room and I pause mid-stir. She's slipped on my shirt from last night. She's rolled the sleeves up and she looks sexy as hell.

"You look much better in that shirt than I do."

"You need your eyes tested, but thank you for the compliment."

She walks over to me and jumps up on the counter. Handing her the coffee, she brings it to her lips and inhales before she takes a sip. Closing her eyes, she moans.

"Good coffee?" I tease.

Her eyes pop open and with a smile that lights up her

face, she nods. "Coffee is life and this here is a ducking good coffee."

"Did you just say ducking?"

"Yeah, I'm used to saying it around Lexi so I now kinda just say it all the time."

Nodding at her, I take a sip. "She really is a great kid." I want to ask about her father, but is it too soon to pry and ask that question? I mean, we've only been on one date and really it's none of my business. Hearing her say my name, snaps my attention back to her. "Sorry, I missed what you said."

"I said, yeah she is, but Mom and Ave are a big part of that."

I decide to go for it. "What about her dad?"

She sighs, "He pops in when he feels like it."

"That's a douche thing to do."

"Well, Creed is a deadbeat so it's no surprises there, but I'd never stop him from seeing her. Just because he and I didn't work out, shouldn't mean she misses out on her father." She looks sad as she says this. "He's actually popping by this afternoon…if he shows."

"He's not reliable?"

She shakes her head, "Not really. I haven't told Lexi because I don't want her to get upset if he bails on her."

"He do that often?"

"More often than not."

"I'm sorry to hear that. Do you need to get home? Or can I offer you brunch?"

"I don't need to be home 'til later so brunch would be lovely. Can I help you cook?"

A laugh breaks free. "I can't cook to save my life, Cress. I was going to order from this little place down the street. They do the best eggs Benny."

"So you do have a flaw?"

"We can't all be perfect, sexy, and amazing like you."

Her cheeks tinge pink at my compliment. I step over to her, take her cup from her hands, and a growl slips through her lips. Gripping her cheeks in my palms, I stare into her eyes before I press my lips to hers. Pulling back, I rest my forehead against hers. "You are exquisite, Cressida Bayliss, don't let anyone tell you otherwise."

Pulling away, I grab the menu from the drawer and hand it to her. "Tell me what you want and I'll order us brunch."

She stares at me. "The Benny sounds amazing, and Preston?" She looks to me. "You're pretty spectacular too."

Wiping my mouth, I lean back in my chair and watch Cress. From the sounds she's currently making, I think she likes the Benny. "It's good, hey?"

"The absolute best. If I died right now, I'd die a happy woman."

"I wouldn't be happy if you died," I say. Pushing back from the table, I walk over to Cress, leaning one hand on the table and sliding the other into her hair, I kiss her temple. "Let's go sit by the pool, you head over and I'll get us another coffee."

She looks up at me. "You had me a coffee."

Racing inside, I make two more coffees and when I head back out, Cress is sitting on the edge of the pool, her legs dangling in the water. Placing the coffees down beside her, I go to take a seat next to her but I lose my balance and fall into the water. When I surface, Cress is laughing; the glee on her face is priceless, and even though I'm wet, that look makes it all worth it.

"Ohhhhhhh, Preston," she says through her laughter. "Are you okay?"

"I'm fine. You should join me, the water is lovely."

"I'm good thanks."

I lunge toward her but she's quicker than me and she rolls to the side, flashing me, and I'm stunned to see she's not wearing any panties. All this time she's been in my shirt and *only* my shirt. Had I known this, I would have taken her on the counter when she first entered the kitchen.

"Where are your panties?" I question, as I pull myself out of the pool. My water soaked my sweats, pulling them low. I notice Cress is staring at me.

"Inside," she nonchalantly says, as she stands up.

"Why are you not wearing them?" She shrugs. "Would you like me to slide my cock into you? Because that is the only reason I can think as to why you would be pantyless right now." I pause and stare at her. Her breathing has become labored and she bites her bottom lip. "I bet you're wet right now."

"I'm not the one who just went for a swim, therefore I'm not wet."

"Not the wetness I'm referring to. I bet you're soaked between your thighs and from the way you just clenched your legs, I bet I'm correct."

"Why don't we take a shower and you can find out?"

Walking over to her, I take her hand in mine and drag her inside. Her phone beeps with a text as we step inside.

"I need to get that, it's Mom's tone."

"I'll go start the shower." Dropping her hand, I slide my arm around her waist and pull her to me. Slamming my lips to her, I kiss her. My tongue slips into her mouth and I kiss her deeply. My hand slips between her thighs and I find her wet and ready. "I knew it," I murmur against her lips. Tapping her on the ass, I turn and walk away, leaving her to check her message.

Turning the water on, I strip off my wet clothes and climb into the shower. Closing my eyes, I step under the flow. Stretching my neck, I smile when I feel her eyes on me. Lifting my head, I can't see through the glass due to the steam. Wiping the glass, Cress comes into view and I cannot believe the sight before me. This woman is the epitome of a sex siren. She reaches behind her and "Closer" by Nine Inch Nails begins to play. Her hips swing from side to side. Her eyes are locked on mine as she lifts her hands and begins to undo the buttons on my shirt. She takes a step forward and spins on her heel. With her back to me, she pulls the shirt down her arms, the material dropping to the tiled floor. She turns back to face me and presses her body against the shower door. Her breasts flattening, she breathes against the glass, fogging it up. She winks at me, steps back, and traces her fingertip around her nipple, the tip hardening from her touch.

"Get in here now, Cress."

She licks her lip and silently opens the door. She steps into the shower stall and under the spray. Water cascades down her body. "Fuck me," I groan. "I love you all wet, Cress."

"Feel free to find out just how wet I am." She lifts her leg and rests it on the shower seat, opening herself to me. Without having to be told twice, I drop to my knees and press my face to her pussy. Flattening my tongue, I lick from taint to clit. She moans, gripping my head in her hands, pressing me farther into her.

"Preston," she mewls. "Please fuck me."

"Not until you come on my tongue."

She lifts her hands and begins to play with her breasts. I watch her hands as I thrust two fingers into her, she's soaked. Taking her clit between my teeth, I gently bite before sucking. I feel her insides clench against my fingers and with a twist, she explodes. Soaking my face with her juices, moaning my name as her orgasm erupts.

Standing up, I stare at her. Both of us heavily breathing, we leap into action together: hands exploring, lips crashing. Tapping her ass, she jumps into my arms and I press her against the wall as she sinks down onto my cock. It's hard. It's fast. It's carnal. We come together, grunting each other's names as we reach our peak.

Lowering her to her feet, we silently stare at one another as we catch our breath. "Can I wash you?" I ask, breaking the silence. She nods her head. Pumping some shower gel into my hands, I soap her up. Paying special attention to her breasts, once she's all cleaned, she returns the favor.

Once we are both clean, we step out. Handing her a towel, we silently dry off. Leaving her to fix her hair, I step into my room and change into jeans and a T-shirt. Cress steps into my room, wrapped in her towel. She drops the towel and pulls on her underwear and dress from last night.

She refastens the halter around her neck and notices me staring at her. "What?"

"Nothing, Love, just admiring your beauty." Her cheeks darken in embarrassment at my compliment. "No need to be embarrassed, Cress. I'm just stating the truth."

"No one has ever made me feel like you do, Preston. It's an odd feeling to be appreciated and wanted."

Stepping over to her, I cup her cheek in my palm. "I will always appreciate you, Cress. Now, let me get you home so you can be ready for your munchkin."

Her eyes light up at the mention of Lexi. "Thank you."

"You are welcome, Love. Now let's go before I strip you out of that dress and make you late." From the look in her eyes, I can tell she'd like that, but I know she needs to get home to her daughter and I'm okay with that. There will always be next time, and I cannot wait for a repeat of last night and this morning.

12 CRESS

Unlocking the front door, I step inside and close it behind me. With a smile on my face, I walk into my bedroom to change into something more appropriate for when Mom drops Lexi home. I don't really want my daughter to see me in last night's dress, that's not a very good example to set.

After changing into capris and a tank, I walk toward the kitchen for a much-needed caffeine boost. While I wait for my coffee, I lean against the counter and images of last night and today flash before my eyes. My body thrumming at the memory of his hands on my body, his cock sliding into me. My mouth on his cock. His tongue in my pussy. His lips on mine. A shudder wracks over my body and then I smell coffee. Looking to the machine, I see my cup of liquid gold waiting for me. Picking up the mug, I bring it to my nose and inhale. The caffeine goodness seeps into my soul. Taking a sip, I close my eyes and moan, a sound I've made many times over the last twelve hours, and sounds I hope to make again this weekend. Preston, Lexi, and I are going to have a picnic on Saturday. Normally I don't want the man I'm sleeping with around Lexi, but there's something about Preston Knight that puts me at ease and allows me to share him with her; there's also the fact she met him the same night I did.

A knock at the door halts that memory. Placing my mug on the countertop I walk to the door, swinging it open, the happiness I just felt dissipates when I see Creed standing before me. His smug face grinning at me. How I ever was in love with this man is beyond me. "Hey."

"Babydoll," he says, leaning forward to kiss my cheek. My body shuddering at his touch. "Where's the squirt?"

"She'll be home soon, you're early," I say, leaning against the door.

"I wanted to see you. Wanted to see if we could squeeze in a quick fuck before I play Daddy." He slides his arm around my waist, pulling me into me. "I know how much you love to fuck."

"Not today," I say, placing my hands on his chest and pushing myself away from him.

"What do you mean not today?" he snarls through clenching teeth.

"Exactly that, not today…or any day again."

He squeezes my shoulders and glares at me, before he viciously shoves me backward. I wasn't expecting it and I stumble, landing on the entrance table. Wincing as the corner jabs my lower left back. Lifting my hand, I rub the spot and cringe. *That's gonna bruise*, I think to myself as I stare at an angry Creed.

"Are you telling me no?" he hisses, spittle flying from his mouth.

"Yes," I defiantly say. It feels good to finally stand up to him. "Creed, we are over. You are Lexi's father and nothing more."

"Are you fucking around on me, Cressida?"

"Whom I sleep with is none of your business, Creed. We have been over for five years now, sure we've occasionally gotten together but that was just a lapse of judgement on my behalf. It won't be happening again."

"Once a slut, always a slut," he retorts, stepping into my face. His hot breath hitting my face, I smell bourbon on his breath and for the first time ever, I don't want Lexi to go with him. "Tell the squirt something came up." With that, he turns around and walks down the path to his car. He climbs in and takes off.

Closing the door, I turn around and lean against the wood, heavily breathing. The fear that built up is slowly ebbing away. The sound of a car door slamming startles me, turning around, I look through the peephole and when I see Mom and Lexi walking up the stairs, I let out the breath I was holding. Swinging the door open, I drop to my knees. "Hey, Munchkin."

"Hey, Mommy."

"How was your day at school?" I ask, my voice wavering a little. Mom notices and looks at me funny, I shake my head subtly but I know, as soon as Lexi is out of earshot, she will be questioning me. *Damn Mom knowing me so well.*

"It was great. Today we learnded all about trains and Trevor got a Woody–" My eyes widen at this. "–and he showed everyone."

My eyes are scrunched in confusion. "Trevor got a Woody?" I question.

She nods excitedly at me. "Yeah, Trevor got a Woody, a big one. You pull Trevor's Woody string and he says all different things. Can we watch *Toy Story* tonight, Mommy?" *Ohh, she's talking about Toy Story.* I stare at her, trying to hold back my laugh. "Can I get a big Woody too?"

"Lex, honey, why don't you go unpack your school bag?" Mom says, and I'm ever so thankful because I'm about to burst out laughing like the big immature kid I am.

"Okay, Nanna."

Lexi walks inside and as soon as she turns down the hallway, the laugh I was holding in erupts. "Oh My God, Mom. How are you not wetting yourself right now?" Mom follows me into the living room and we take a seat on the sofa.

"Because I'm worried about you. What happened? Where's Creed?"

At the mention of Creed, my laughter stops. I stare at Mom and the fear from earlier comes back. "He's an ass."

"No shit, Sherlock. What did Dickwad do now?"

"Ruined my good mood." She eyes me. "It's fine, he just showed his true colors. He won't be spending the afternoon with Lexi."

"Well, that's a bonus. The less time she spends with him the better. He's—"

"Moooom," I interrupt. "He's her father."

"Just 'cause she has his DNA, that does not make him a father. It just makes him a sperm donor and thankfully for us, there's more Bayliss DNA in her than Dawson DNA. Enough about Dickwad, tell me all about last night?"

My lips lift in a smile as I think about Preston and last night.

"Now *that's* the look I love to see on your face," Mom says. "That is the look I want to see after you spend time with a man."

"Mom." I swat at her arm.

"Sooo, how was it?"

Thankfully Lexi comes back into the room and jumps on the sofa between us, saving me from the Spanish Inquisition…for now. Mom is not just my mom, she's also my best friend. We probably tell each other more than necessary, but after Dad died and it was just the two of us, we became a team.

Lexi is still talking about Trevor's big Woody and I'm still biting my tongue holding back my laugh. Mom brings up Netflix and turns the movie on. We end up watching one and two, with a promise to watch the rest after school tomorrow. Mom leaves, without getting the answers she wants, but I know that when I get back from dropping Lexi at school tomorrow, Mom will be waiting with coffee and cake for a gossip session.

After a hot relaxing shower, I climb into bed. Wincing when I lay down, my lower back is really sore and it's already started to bruise. I'm just about asleep when my phone beeps with a text. Grabbing it off the bedside table, I smile, it's from Preston.

PRESTON: *Nite nite, Love. I can smell you on my pillow, it's my new favorite scent.*

PRESTON: *Is it Saturday yet?*

CRESS: *It's almost Saturday.*

CRESS: *My pillow smells like Tide*

PRESTON: *Maybe I need to come over and rub myself all over your pillow*

CRESS: *I'd rather you rub me but if pillows are your thing, who am I to stop you?*

PRESTON: *Flirty minx…now I'm hard*

CRESS: *Do you have a big Woody?*

I laugh to myself at my reply. I will never be able to think of *Toy Story* and Woody the same again...and I won't be able to look at little Trevor the same either. That kid has scarred me for life.

> **PRESTON:** *Whenever I think about you, I always sport a big Woody...have you forgotten already? Do we need a repeat of last night to refresh your mind?*
> **CRESS:** *My memory is just fine, but I'm down with a repeat...I do love to tango, vertically AND horizontally*
> **PRESTON:** *Dammit, Cress, I was just texting to say goodnight*
> **CRESS:** *Goodnight, Dr. Knight*
> **PRESTON:** *Goodnight, Ms. Bayliss*

With a smile on my face, I drift off to sleep dreaming about Preston's big woody and how he makes me reach for the sky.

13 PRESTON

D̲ue to an emergency at the hospital, I had to cancel my picnic plans with Cress and Lexi. Thankfully, she was understanding. Previous girlfriends would always get angry if I cancelled short notice, but not Cress. She wished me the best and said we'd catch up soon.

It's early evening when I finally get home, I'm absolutely exhausted but I want to check in with Cress. Grabbing a beer, I fall onto the sofa, put on *DuckTales*, take a sip, and message Cress.

PRESTON: *Just got home, I'm shattered*

CRESS: *Glad you're home safely. How was your day?*

PRESTON: *Long and hard*

CRESS: *I was asking about your day, not your cock **wink wink***

PRESTON: *You dirty girl…I think you need a spanking*

CRESS: *I'm down with that **spank spank** **wink wink***

Man, this woman continues to amaze me. She comes across as a saint but underneath she's a dirty, dirty girl… and I love it. I'm currently picturing Cress bent over my sofa; her ass in the air and it's pink with an imprint of my hand. Fuck, now my cock is hard.. Looking at the television, I see that *DuckTales* is finished and now *Scooby Doo* is on, and I have to say it's my all-time favorite cartoon. Scooby and Shaggy begin to eat a really gross sandwich, but the inner child in me kinda wants to see what it tastes like too and with that, my cock is no longer long and hard.

PRESTON: *Watcha doing?*
CRESS: *Eating pizza and ice cream with Lexi*
PRESTON: *I like pizza and ice cream*
CRESS: *Who doesn't?*
PRESTON: *I'd like to eat it off of your naked body*
CRESS: *Oh. I'm game for that…maybe for our next date?*
PRESTON: *When and where? I'm there*
PRESTON: *Plus I owe you a spanking*

She doesn't respond straightaway and I find myself disappointed. Texting with Cress is fast becoming my favorite pastime.

CRESS: *Sorry, had to get Lexi to bed. Now tell me more about this ice cream eating and spanking*

I smile at her response and my cock likes it too. I would love nothing more than to drive over to her place, grab some mint chocolate chip ice cream along the way and do exactly that. "Fuuuuck," I groan as I readjust my cock.

PRESTON: *Well…it would involve you naked, a tub of ice cream and my tongue…licking said ice cream off every inch of your body. Then I'd slap your ass 'til it's red. Once it's glowing, I'll let you suck ice cream off my cock, and then I'd fuck you into the wee hours of the morning.*

CRESS: *Why, Dr. Knight, you are one dirty doc.*

PRESTON: *You wouldn't have me any other way*

PRESTON: *Care to have that picnic with me tomorrow? And maybe I can make the above a reality…my cock and I would very much like that*

CRESS: *As much as I would love part two, rain check on that one. As for option one, we will pick you up at 11*

PRESTON: *It's a date and a rain check*

CRESS: *Good night, Dr. Knight*

PRESTON: *Be sweet, parakeet*

CRESS: *That's totally corny*

PRESTON: *You love it*

CRESS: *Yeah, I kinda do. Nite, Preston*

PRESTON: *Nite, Love*

Finishing off my beer, I pop the empty into the recycling and crawl into bed. I'm asleep before my head hits the pillow and all too soon, my alarm is blaring. Climbing out of bed, I grab a shower and like I have all week, I remember the striptease Cress gave me last weekend. I love that she brings out her wild side with me, and her wild side meshes with mine like peas and carrots. She's the complete perfect package. She's messing with my head but hell; I'm going to do my best to hold on to her.

Stretching my arms over my head, I stretch out my tight muscles. I slept like the dead last night, and today, I feel refreshed and excited for my picnic with Cress and Lexi. Showering quickly, I pull on a pair of cargos, a Metallica T-shirt, and my Chucks. Looking at the clock, I see I still have an hour until they get here so I make myself a coffee and head out back to enjoy the morning sun. I'm totally zoned out when the doorbell rings.

Hopping up, I pop my mug on the counter and head toward the door. Swinging it open, I'm met with a smiling Cress and an anxious looking Lexi. "Good morning, ladies."

"He called me a lady," Lexi whispers to Cress.

"Then you better act like one," Cress tells her daughter.

"Good day, kind sir," Lexi says, looking to her mom with a big grin on her face. "May I do poo poo in your toilet?"

"Lexi," Cress scoffs, her cheeks darkening with embarrassment.

"It's fine, Love." I offer my hand to Lexi. "Follow me, Munchkin."

"Thank you, kind sir."

Holding back a laugh, we walk inside. Looking over my shoulder, I see Cress still standing in the doorway. "You coming?" As soon as the words are out of my mouth, I realize it sounded dirty.

Cress winks at me. "Why thank you, kind sir, I'd love to." Then she mouths 'later' back at me.

"Minx," I whisper.

"What's a minx?" Lexi asks, clearly I said it louder than I intended.

"Ummm, ahh…it's a—"

I stumble as to what to say but, thankfully, Cress walks over to us and puts her hand on Lexi's shoulder and guides her toward the bathroom. "Come on, Munchkin, let's go poo poo."

Just like that, my faux pas is forgotten...that is until I hear, "Mommy, what's a minx?"

"Less talking, more pooping," I hear Cress say to Lexi. I laugh again, you'd think after dealing with kids all day, every day, I'd be more careful, but when I'm around Cress, all rational thought evaporates and I become a bumbling teenager again. The Cress effect is strong when she's around.

"You have a pool?" Lexi screams, racing to the windows looking out to the backyard. She turns to Cress, her little face lit up like a Christmas tree. "Can we go swimming, Mommy?"

"I thought you wanted a picnic in the park?" Cress says to her, as she walks over to me.

"I want a pool picnic now. Can we, Mom? Can we?"

"I don't—"

"I'm happy to do that, if it's okay with you?"

"Are you sure?"

Nodding my head. "Not a problem at all...but do you two have suits?"

"Ohh no," Lexi dramatically says. "I don't," she dejectedly sighs.

"I have a suggestion." They both look to me. "There's a mall at the end of the street, what if we go get some swimsuits and stuff for our picnic, then we can come back here and start our pool picnic."

"That be tabolous. Can we, Mommy? Pleeeeeease?"

"Yeah, Mommy, can we, Mommy? Pleeeeeease?" I mimic Lexi, she looks to me and grins. Her smile melts my heart.

"Sounds like a plan to me, let's go."

An hour later, we are back at the house. Everyone has new swimwear and we have a gourmet feast to dine upon after our swim.

Lexi and Cress change in the spare room and I change in mine. I'm getting drinks together when I hear a giggle coming down the hallway. Lexi and Cress step into the room and my eyes bug open. Cress is wearing a sexy as hell, bright orange one-piece with cutouts on the sides. Lexi is wearing a pink and purple *My Little Pony*—surprise surprise—one piece.

"Can we please go swimming now, Dr. Preston?"

"As long as it's okay with Mommy?"

"Let's do this," she says, taking Lexi's hand she leads her out back.

My eyes drop to Cress's ass as they walk past. "That ass," I whisper, but again, it clearly wasn't as quiet as I'd hoped because Cress looks back at me. With a wink, she turns and keeps walking, with an added sway to her hips.

"Fuuuuck," I growl, subtly adjusting my cock.

"You coming?" Cress sasses as she opens the slider. She escorts Lexi outside, again emphasizing the swish of her hips.

"Fucking minx," I whisper to myself, shaking my head and grinning like the lovesick fool I am.

Grabbing our drinks, I head out and join them.

Cress is rubbing sunscreen on Lexi and I get excited at the prospect of rubbing sunscreen on Cress, but much to my disappointment, she leaps into the pool. Her body slicing through the water, she breaks the surface and I watch as water cascades down her body. "Your turn, Munchkin," Cress says to Lexi, who's standing on the edge.

She shakes her head. "I can't jump like you, Mommy."

Stepping beside her, I crouch down. "How about we jump together?" She shakes her head, her little body shaking with fear. It's the first time I've seen the vivacious little girl not going at it with everything she has. "What if we wade in from over there?" I point to the shallow kiddie area. I love this pool for that, I actually spend most of my time sitting in the shallow end, leaning back and enjoying a beer.

She nods her head at me and slips her hand into mine. Standing back up, we walk over to the area. I step down first so she can see how deep it is. A slight smile appears on her face as she climbs in, her face beaming when the water touches her. She immediately drops herself down, just her head hovering above the water. She stands up and walks to the edge before it drops off and looks to Cress.

"Having fun, Munchkin?"

She nods her head and the next minute, she's leaping through the air toward Cress, dive-bombing in front of her mother. Cress grins at Lexi when she resurfaces, the two of them laughing with joy. The sound is music to my ears and I find myself grinning as I watch them splash about together.

Cress looks over at me, and the smile on her face gets my heart racing. "That didn't take long," I say, nodding to Lexi who is paddling around the pool.

"She totally suckered you. This one is a water baby," Cress says, as she throws Lexi up in the air. She squeals in delight before she crashes to the water.

Shuffling to the edge, I dangle my feet over and watch the two of them swim about. I don't get out here as much as I would like and it's great to see it being used. Cress and Lexi swim toward me. Lexi climbs onto the ledge and sits next to me. Cress rests her hands on my thighs and lifts herself up. She places a quick kiss on my lips. I'm shocked that she would do that in front of Lexi.

Reaching out, I grip her hips in my hands and she hisses in pain, pulling away from me.

"Are you hurt?" I question as she jumps up and sits next to me.

She vehemently shakes her head. "I'm fine," she says, but I notice her hand resting on her lower back.

"Cress," I warn, "what's wrong?"

She looks to Lexi, when she sees that she's occupied blowing bubbles, she leans to the side and pulls one of the cutouts away from her body. My eyes pop wide open at what I see and my blood boils.

14   CRESS

"WHAT THE FUCK, CRESS?" HE GROWLS, ANGER RADIATING from him but it's not at me, it's for me.

"Language," I scoff, hoping to take the attention away from my back.

"What the duck, Cress? What the duck happened?"

"Nothing, it was an accident," I plead.

"Don't ducking lie to me, Cress. What happened?"

Sighing, I shake my head and close my eyes. "Not now."

"Creeesss."

I look to Lexi and he understands and nods his head. "Later you will tell me who hurt you."

"Promise."

"I'm hungry, Mommy."

"Me too," Preston says. "How about we hop out? I'll fire up the grill and then after we eat, we can watch a movie."

"Yes, yes, yes," Lexi excitedly says, splashing about in glee.

"Okay, you two, hang in the pool and I'll go cook."

Preston steps out of the pool and I stare as he climbs out. Water sluicing down his body. His muscles flexing in that delicious way. *Man, he's hot*, I think to myself as I watch him dry off. I want to be that towel. He looks over at me and notices me staring at him, he smiles but it doesn't reach his eyes like it usually does. He's angry about the bruise. To be honest, I forgot about it. It isn't sore anymore but when I bump it, or someone squeezes me, it hurts like a bitch. *Fucking Creed*, ruining things once again for me.

Not wanting to dwell on things, I focus on Lexi. Sitting on the edge of the pool, I kick my legs back and forth watching her. She's beaming right now, jumping and splashing. I wasn't joking earlier when I said she's a water baby—I'm pretty sure she was a mermaid in a past life.

Looking over my shoulder, I watch as Preston lights the grill. His face is laced with concern and I'm the cause of that. I need to talk to him and put him at ease, but I know this man, he's going to go all alpha and lose his shit when I tell him what happened. I know he cares but I can handle Creed. I don't want, or need, him getting involved in this.

With a sigh, I look back to my water baby. "Lexi, baby, time to hop out."

"Please, Mom, can I stay for a little longer?"

"If you are a good girl, I'm sure you can have another swim after lunch. Why don't you get your iPad and watch some Pony while I help Preston with lunch?"

"Okay, Mommy." She kicks her way over to me and I help her out of the water. Wrapping her in a towel, I pull out her headphones and iPad. She walks over to the outdoor lounger near the grill and reclines back. Handing her the device, she focuses on the screen and is transported to Equestria with her pony friends.

Walking over to Preston, I stand next to him. "Please don't be mad at me." I place my hand on his back, hoping to calm him with my touch.

He looks to me and shakes his head. "I'm not mad at you, I'm mad that someone did this to you."

"How do you know I didn't do it to myself?" He eyes me in a 'I'm-not-a-fool-don't-treat-me-like-a-fool' way. "Fine," I huff, crossing my arms across my chest defiantly, as I rest against the grill bench. "The other day when Creed came to see Lexi, he wanted to hook up." His eyes pop wide open and he clenches his jaw, I shake my head from side to side, "I told him no, and he didn't like it. I stepped back from him and hit the corner of the hall table."

"You stepped back? Or he pushed you?"

"A little of both."

"Cress, why are you defending him?"

"Because it's nothing. He was mad I wouldn't sleep with him."

"You were still sleeping with him?"

"Occasionally I would, yes, but I haven't slept with him in over a year. Ave would always yell at me when I would and after I always felt ashamed. When I saw him the other day, I felt nothing for him." Taking a deep breath, I continue, "For the first time ever, he didn't have a hold on me. It felt freeing and clearly I pissed him off. I don't think he meant to hurt me."

"Don't defend his actions, Cress. You never, N-E-V-E-R hit a woman."

"He didn't hit me."

"Hit, push, whatever. You never touch a woman, period."

"Well, I guess you won't be touching me ever again," I tease.

He slides his hand around my waist, pulls me into him, and whispers, "How I touch you is the *only* way a woman should be touched." He kisses my neck. "Every inch of their body should be worshipped." Kiss. "Caressed." Kiss. "Admired." Kiss. "Adored." Kiss. "Loved."

Swallowing deeply, I stare up at him. "I like how you worship, adore, caress, and love my body." Looking over his shoulder, I see that Lexi isn't looking; lifting to my toes, I press my lips to his and kiss him deeply. Wrapping my arms around his shoulders, I press myself into his body. His cock thickens between us. Pulling back, I grin, "Seems you like how I worship you too."

"You are a minx, Cress Bayliss. Just you wait 'til I get you alone."

"Ohh yeah, and what will you do to me, Preston Knight?"

"Well." He leans in, his breath heating my neck. He nibbles my earlobe and whispers, "First, I would strip you out of this sexy as fuck one-piece. Then I would lick and worship every inch of your body with my tongue. Then I'd pay extra attention to your pussy with my mouth and fingers and once you'd come on my face, I'd fuck you. I'd fuck you hard and fast and after you've come again, I'd fuck you sweetly and slowly."

My body is thrumming as I process his words. My clit throbs. "Preston, you don't play fair."

"All's fair in orgasms and war," he says. He kisses the tip of my nose and turns away to focus on the grill.

"Asshole," I mumble under my breath. "I'll go get us more drinks and the sides."

"Okay," he says, without a care in the world.

As I walk away from him, I grin as an evil thought appears. Grabbing my phone off the counter, I race into the bathroom and lock the door; I really don't want Lexi to walk in on this. Lifting my leg onto the vanity, I slide my finger under my suit, I accidentally brush my clit. I shudder and moan at the contact. "Damn you, Preston," I whisper.

Positioning my phone, I take a sexy pic of my finger under my suit and text it to Preston.

CRESS: *Payback's a bitch*
CRESS: ***attaches photo***

Washing my hands, I head into the kitchen and prepare the salad to go with the chicken breasts. I'm grabbing the plates when my phone pings with a text. Looking up, I see Preston staring at me. With a smirk, I read his reply.

PRESTON: *You are a minx…your ass is mine next time we are alone*
CRESS: *What is your obsession with my ass?*
PRESTON: *Have you seen your ass? How can I not be an ass man?*

A laugh breaks free at his reply and another evil thought once again appears. Pulling my one-piece up into my ass crack, I lean over the counter to enhance my ass, and quickly snap a pic.

CRESS: ***attaches photo***

From where I'm standing, I hear Preston moan. *Score one, Cress,* I think to myself as I carry out the salad and plates. Placing them on the table, I wink at Preston and walk over to Lexi. "Let's go wash up for lunch, Munchkin."

"Can I finish this episode first?"

"Nope, hands now, missy."

"Fine," she huffs.

Turning off her iPad, she places it on the table and I follow her inside. We are in the bathroom washing her hands, when I think about what I did in here just a few moments ago, my cheeks darken and I shudder.

Once our hands are sparkly clean, we grab some drinks and head back outside to join Preston. He's dishing up and seeing him all domesticated causes another shiver to wrack through my body.

"Mmmmm, smells great," I say, as I push Lexi's chair in.

He winks at me and takes his seat, handing me my plate. Our fingers brush and an electrical current zaps through me, my already pulsing clit now throbs. I swallow a moan but Preston notices, he smirks at me and I mouth 'asshole' at him.

After lunch, we laze in the kiddie part of the pool. The day has been amazing. Preston and Lexi get along like a house on fire, watching them together makes my heart happy. We have one final swim and then we head inside to clean up and watch a movie.

Lexi and Preston are sitting on the sofa arguing over

which Pony is the best. With a smile on my face, I leave them to it and set about loading the dishwasher and tidying up. It's only fair since Preston cooked.

Closing the dishwasher, I step into the living room to join them and I stop mid-step. The scene before me is gorgeous and takes my breath away. *My Little Pony* is on the TV, Preston and Lexi are both on the sofa. He's lying on the chaise and Lexi is snuggled into his side, his arm wrapped around her and both of them are sound asleep. Someone's snoring and I think it might be my daughter. Clearly all the swimming took it out of them both.

Grabbing my phone off the counter, I snap a photo and set it as my screen lock photo. I've just set it when my phone pings with a text.

CREED: *I'm at your place, where the fuck are you?*
CRESS: *Out*
CREED: *When will you be home?*
CRESS: *Later*
CREED: *I want to see Lexi. Get your ass home now*
CRESS: *I'll be home later. How about tomorrow?*
CREED: *I want to see her now. Get the fuck back here now, bitch*
CRESS: *We will be home later.*
CREED: *You better be or I will see to it that she lives elsewhere*
CRESS: *Don't threaten me, Creed*
CREED: *Or what? Huh?*

Shaking my head, I sigh in frustration. I know not to engage him otherwise we will just go round and round in circles. Him threating to take Lexi has really pissed me off but it's also scared me, he's never threatened that before.

CRESS: *We will see you tomorrow, Creed*
CREED: *Make sure the squirt is ready when I get there*

Dropping my phone back onto the countertop, I rest my hands on the edge, lower my head, and sigh. My heart is racing right now. I know I've enraged Creed but he needs to know I'm not at his beck and call anymore...I just hope I haven't pushed him too far.

15 PRESTON

After my little catnap with Lexi, I look over to see Cress sitting in the armchair. I lie here and watch her for a few moments, she's deep in thought and I don't like the look on her face. Carefully, I ease Lexi off me and I walk over to Cress. Sitting on the coffee table, I place my hand on her knee and she jumps six feet in fright.

"Shit, Preston, you scared me."

"What's wrong? You were so deep in thought you didn't even see me walk over here."

"I'm fine."

I scoff, "Cress, when a woman says she's fine, she is anything but. What's happened?"

She picks up her phone and hands it to me. Scrolling through the text thread, I read the messages from Creed, my blood boiling with each message I see. "He's threatening you?" She nods at me. "Has he done this before?" She shakes her head. "Cress, are you worried?"

She looks up at me and sadly nods, a tear cascades

down her cheek. She looks so frightened right now. "Preston, he's threatening to take Lexi from me, how can I not be worried? She's my everything, Preston."

"I won't let that happen," I say.

Standing up, I lift Cress up, sit down and place her on my lap. Hugging her tightly to me, her body shuddering with fear. Kissing her temple, I run my hand soothingly up and down her leg. Resting my head against hers, I ask, "Tell me what I can do."

"This works for now." She snuggles farther into me.

"What's wrong, Mommy?" Lexi asks.

We both look up to see Lexi staring at us.

"Nothing, Munchkin, just snuggling," Cress says, any hint of her fear hidden from her daughter. She really is a remarkable mom.

"Can I snuggle too?" she asks.

"I don't think so," Cress says, while at the same time I say, "Sure, come on up, Munchkin."

Cress lifts her head and looks at me, while Lexi takes the opportunity and climbs onto my lap too. She snuggles in and the three of us sit here in silence.

"I like this," Cress murmurs.

"Me too," I confirm, placing a kiss on her head.

"And me, don't forget me," Lexi adds.

"How could we forget you, Princess?"

"You think I'm a princess?" she asks

"All good little girls are a princess, right, Cress?"

"Exactly," Cress agrees. "I was a princess when I was your age too."

"What are you now, Mommy?"

"A queen," I reply.

Cress lifts her head and stares at me, for the first time since I woke up, she smiles and it reaches her eyes.

"Well, where's my crown?" Lexi asks.

Cress and I both laugh. "Well, we better do something about that then," I say, "Next time I'm in the crown store, I'll get you one."

"And one for Mommy," Lexi says. "A queen needs a crown too."

"I will be sure to get two of their finest crowns."

"Good," Lexi says. "Can I have a lollipop, Mommy?"

"Of course, you can grab one from my bag."

She hopes off my lap and races away. I watch as she skips off, without a care in the world. Ohh to be five years old again. She returns with three lollipops and hands them to us. "Can you open this for me please, Dr. Preston?" she asks, as she climbs back onto me.

"Of course, and you know you can just call me Preston," I say, as I open the wrapper and hand it back to her.

"I know," she says matter-of-factly, "but you are my doctor friend."

"Can't argue with that," Cress adds, as she slides the candy into her mouth…my mind goes to dirty town and I remember that blowjob from the other morning. From the look in her eyes, she knows exactly what she's doing.

'Minx,' I mouth to her.

She shrugs and continues to suck the lollipop as if she was sucking my cock. My cock twitches, he feels each and every suck and lick. A low groan builds in the back of my throat.

"Mommy, I think we are crushing Dr. Preston. We should hop off him. He groanded."

My eyes widen because if Cress hops off, my cock will be standing to attention and that's the last thing I need, or want, Lexi to see.

"It's fine," I say. "I like having you two in my arms."

They both nod. The three of us quietly sit here. The moment is perfect.

"Wanna suck?" Lexi asks, offering me up her lollipop.

I shake my head side to side, "Thanks, but I prefer pink ones."

Cress scoffs and shakes her head.

"I like pink ones too but I prefer purple ones," Lexi says, popping the sucker back into her mouth.

"How about you, Cress?" I look down at her. "What do you prefer to suck?"

"I like hard purple ones," she says, her eyes locked on mine as she says this. I subtly shake my head at her.

"Me too, Mommy, can I get a hard purple one?"

Cress and I both burst out laughing, not wanting to be left out, Lexi laughs too. This makes me laugh harder. "Who knew lollipops could be so funny?"

"And dirty," Cress quietly adds.

Lexi hears the theme song to *My Little Pony* and she leaps off my lap, dives onto the sofa, and watches the TV intently. Completely forgetting about hard purple lollipops.

"Wow, she really does love that show."

"You have no idea," Cress replies.

We hop up and join Lexi on the sofa. Cress snuggles into my side and Lexi snuggles into her. Absentmindedly I play with her hair, her body relaxes into me and I smile. She was so worked up earlier due to the messages from Creed, it's nice to see her back to normal. But if I'm honest, those messages scare me. I know Cress is tough, but this Creed guy seems crazy and I fear for her and Lexi. I know she wants Lexi to see her father but if he's like this, I think she'd be better off without him. It's not my place to say anything so for now, I'll bite my tongue but if things continue, I'll step in. I care deeply for Cress and Lexi, and I won't let anything happen to them.

They have just left, I had such a great time today and Lexi is a little firecracker, but then again, Cress is her mom so I wouldn't expect anything else. Popping the last of the dishes into the dishwasher, I turn it on and head into my bedroom and get ready for bed. I have a morning shift tomorrow so I need an early night.

Lying down, I stare at the ceiling, sleep eludes me right now. My phone pings with a text, picking it up I smile when I see it's from Cress.

CRESS: *Thank you for a wonderful day. Lexi and I had a great time*

PRESTON: *My pleasure. I had a ball too. Look forward to doing it again*

CRESS: *It? or me?*

PRESTON: *You are such a minx, I'm pretty sure you know what I want to do*

CRESS: *I may need a reminder*

PRESTON: *Next time we are alone, I will show you **wink wink***

PRESTON: *PS. When can I get another tango lesson?*

CRESS: *Soon, grasshopper, soon…you are my most favorite dance partner*

PRESTON: *Well, YOU are my most favorite person when it comes to persons*

CRESS: *Aww, you say the sweetest things. Nite, Preston*

PRESTON: *Nite Nite, Queen Cress*

Placing my phone down, I hop up and grab my Mac. I

quickly order a present for my two royal ladies. I wish I could be there when they open them, but if I know Cress, she will send me a pic. With a smile on my face, I drift off to sleep, happy and content. My life is pretty perfect right now, nothing can bring me down.

16   CRESS

A FEW DAYS AFTER OUR AMAZING DAY AT PRESTON'S, a package arrives addressed to Princess Lexi and Queen Cress. Popping it on the dining table, I decide to wait until Lexi is home from school and we will open it together. I've finished mopping the floors when there's another knock at the door. Looking through the peephole, I sigh when I see it's Creed on the other side.

Opening the door, I put on a fake smile. "Hey, Creed."

"Dollface," he replies, the sound of his voice grating on my nerves. "Where's the squid?"

"At school."

"Ohh, thought she'd be home."

"Creed, you know she finishes at 11:45 a.m."

"I have an idea as to what we can do to pass the time." He winks suggestively at me.

"Thanks, but no thanks."

"Are you turning me down again? A slut like you always wants a piece of this." He grabs his junk and thrusts his hips toward me. "Come on, Dollface, it's been ages since I sank myself inside of your cunt."

"Creed," I warn, and just like the other week, he steps inside. He backs me into the wall, I have nowhere to go. He rests his hands either side of my head and licks along my jawbone.

"I forgot how good your skin tastes," he says, sliding this pinky down my neck.

Closing my eyes, I shudder and thankfully, a car door slamming in my driveway startles him and he pulls back. A few seconds later, Mom walks inside. Never have I been so thankful for her to pop in unannounced.

"Cress, everything okay?"

Nodding my head, I smile but I know Mom realizes it's fake. "Yeah, all good, Mom. I was just telling Creed that Lexi is still at school. I was about to offer for him to meet us at the park after I've picked her up, but you arrived before I could do that."

"Yes, it would be lovely for you to join us," Mom says, her voice void of any emotion.

"If she'll be there," he flicks his finger toward Mom, "I'll pass." He looks back at me. "Cress, you and I will fuck soon, there's no stopping it. You know it as well as I do. Just give it to me and then everyone wins."

He turns on his heel and leaves. Mom slams the door behind him and I let out the breath that I was holding.

"You okay, baby?" Mom says, stepping to me, she rests her hand on my arm; her touch instantly calms me.

Nodding, I lie, "Yeah, I'm fine."

Pulling Mom into a hug, I hold on to her. My body shaking as the fear slowly fades. Mom hugs me back and whispers, "Please talk to me, sweetheart." She pulls back and grips my cheeks in that mom way.

"It's fine, Mom. Creed is just being Creed."

She nods but she knows I'm lying, she also knows I won't talk until I'm ready, but I don't want to talk about this. Not now, not ever.

It's fine.

Everything will be fine.

But even as I tell myself this, I know it's far from the truth. Creed Dawson is a mean, narcissistic son of a bitch at the best of times, and I have just severely pissed him off. This is now the second time I've rejected him, but it's the first time I have stood my ground with him. I hope I haven't wakened the beast.

Mom helps me finish cleaning the house and then we go pick Lexi up. Lexi is excited to see Mom with me and we stop off at the park, just like I suggested to Creed earlier. I keep expecting to see him here too, but at the moment, he'll be fuming and pissed off. Lexi will be the last thing on his mind, and I'm grateful for that. Never before have I not wanted him to see her, but now I don't want him anywhere near my daughter.

The time at the park is a blur, I'm thankful Mom was with us. My mind wasn't where it should have been, focusing on my daughter. If anything had of happened to her because I was lost in my head, I would never forgive myself. Lexi is my everything and I will do everything in my power to protect her, that's my job as her mom and it's a job I take seriously.

When we walk in the door, Lexi immediately sees the box on the table. She points to it. "What's that, Mommy?"

"It's a package for us," I tell her.

She squeals in delight. "I never get presents unless it's my birthday or Christmas. What is it?"

"I don't know, how about we open it and see?"

"Yes!" she screams in excitement and races to the table, pulls out the chair, and climbs up. She drags the box to her and pretends to read the label. "What does it say, Mommy?"

"It has our address on it and it's addressed to, Princess Lexi and Queen Cress."

"That's us. Dr. Preston called us Princess and Queen on the weekend."

"It might be from him then," I tell her.

"Let's open it, let's open it," she squeals in delight, the sheer joy on her face is priceless right now.

Pulling at the tape, we open the box. Lexi pulls back the flaps and her eyes widen. "Ohh, Mommy, I'm a real princess now."

Peeking over her shoulder, I see two plastic crowns. A smile graces my face and I shake my head. "Preston," I murmur to myself.

"Can we wear them?" Lexi excitedly asks, her body buzzing with excitement.

"How about we have our shower and then we can?"

"Okay…and can we call Prince Dr. Preston to say thank you?"

"We can try but he might be at work."

"Deal." She jumps down from the table and races into the bathroom. First time ever she hasn't argued when I've told her to have a shower.

An hour later, we are both freshly showered, in our pajamas, and wearing our crowns. The lasagna is in the oven warming and we are watching, surprise, surprise, *My Little Pony.*

"Can we call Prince Dr. Preston?" Lexi asks as the cartoon comes to an end.

"Sure," I say. Leaning forward I grab my phone and bring up Preston's contact details.

"Can we Face call instead?"

"We can try."

Lexi settles on my lap and we call Preston. He answers immediately and I smile when I see he's shirtless, his chest glistening with sweat. "Thank you, Prince Dr. Preston, I love my crown," Lexi says before he can even say hello.

"You are most welcome, Princess Lexi. You look beautiful."

"What about Queen Mommy?"

"Queen Cress is also beautiful."

"Why thank you, Prince Preston," I say, bowing my head down. He winks at me and even though I'm in my nightie wearing a plastic crown, I do feel beautiful. The hungry look in Preston's eyes sets my insides ablaze.

"No, Mommy, he's Prince Dr. Preston."

"Ohh, I'm sorry, thank you, Prince Dr. Preston."

"I'll let it slide just this time since you both look stunning in your crowns."

The oven beeps and Lexi wriggles in my lap. "Dinner's ready. Bye," she says, jumping down from my lap.

"Guess that means I have to go." He nods. "Thank you again for our crowns."

"Maybe you can wear it for me sometime…only that."

"That can be arranged."

"Mooooooom," Lexi sings from the kitchen.

"I'll talk to you soon."

Hanging up from Preston, I pop my phone down. I am

totally falling for Dr. Knight and I'm pretty sure, he's falling for me too. Walking into the kitchen, I turn the oven timer off. Taking out the lasagna, I dish it up. Lexi and I eat at the dining table, proudly wearing our crowns and pretending to be royals.

Over the next few weeks, the taunts from Creed increase. From the horrible text messages to the verbal lashings I get each time he's here to collect Lexi, he's progressively getting worse. And to top it off, when Lexi gets home from spending time with him, her behavior and language is atrocious. She has never acted out like this before.

Hopping out of the shower, I pull on my jean shorts and a white linen long-sleeved shirt and roll the sleeves up. Looking at the clock, I see that Creed will be here soon to pick Lexi up. She's excited and beaming because today he's taking her to the circus. That's one outing I'm happy for them to do together because well, clowns. Those smiling assholes give me the heebie-jeebies, being trapped inside a tent with them is NOT my idea of fun.

There's a knock at the door and Lexi races to answer it. She opens it and Creed is standing there. Leaning against the doorframe as if his shit don't stink and I can tell from the look on his face, we are going to fight before they leave.

"Daddy Creeeeed," Lexi excitedly says.

"Dollface," he says to me, my skin tingling and not in the sexy way it does with Preston. I notice that he doesn't greet Lexi, or get angry at the 'Daddy Creed' tag.

"Her name is Mommy or Queen Mommy."

"Like fuck she's a queen," he sneers at Lexi.

"Please don't speak to her like that."

"I'll talk to *MY* daughter however the fuck I want. Get your things, Squid, we're gonna be late."

Lexi turns and skips to her room to get her shoes and jacket, unaware of what's about to unravel between Creed and I.

"Creed," I warn when I know that Lexi isn't in earshot, she doesn't need to see us argue. "You—"

"What? What the fuck do you have to say? Finally wanting a piece of this?" He thrusts his hips and points to his cock.

"I'll pass, thanks."

Clearly this pisses him off because he steps inside and slams me into the wall. "One of these days, slut, you are going to beg me to fuck you and I'll fuck you good. Sluts like you like it hard and fast and rough. I'm getting hard just thinking about slamming my cock into your cunt. Strangling you as I pound into you. Watching the oxygen seep out of your body as I continue to fuck you like you've never been fucked before. Sluts like you love being fucked like that."

"Mommy," Lexi says from the entry to the hallway.

Shoving Creed off me, I swallow deeply and drop down to my knees. I stare at her and smile. I want to change my mind about letting her go with him but I know that deep down, he will never hurt her. His issue is with me, not her. "You have a good time at the circus with Creed."

"Daddy," he snarls from above us. First time ever that he wants to be called Daddy, what's up with him? His behavior is very odd at the moment.

"Creed will drop you home after the circus." Placing a kiss on her head, she hugs me and leaves with Creed.

Closing the door, I lean my head against the wood and

the tears begin to fall. I need Preston. On autopilot, I grab my bag and keys, jump into my car, and drive over to his place. Walking up to his front door, I ring the bell. A few moments later it opens and as soon as I see Preston, I launch myself at him. Wrapping my arms around his neck.

"Cress, Love, what's wrong?"

"Please just hold me," I say as I cry into his neck. I hold on to him for dear life, he's the lifeline I need right now. Without saying anything, he lifts me into his arms and carries me bridal style inside. He sits down on the sofa and hugs me tighter to him. Nuzzling my head into his neck, I continue to cry. I'm a sobbing mess right now and I can't stop, the floodgates have opened and they are pouring out.

Placing his fingers under my chin, he lifts my head so I'm looking at him. "Cress, Love, you're scaring me."

Nodding my head, I sniff and stare at him. Still unable to speak.

He wipes his thumb under my eyes, wiping away my tears but as soon as the skin is dry, new tears wet it again. Lowering my head to his shoulder, I close my eyes and hold on to him. His embrace and kisses on my head calm me.

The tears finally stop, lifting my head, I stare at him. He cups my cheek in his palm, I lean into his touch. "What do you need, Love?"

"You," I whisper. "I just need you."

17 PRESTON

"You, I just need you." She wraps her arms around me tighter.

Lifting her head, she sadly smiles, leans forward, and presses her lips to mine. Gripping her cheeks in my palms, I kiss her back. Pouring everything I have into this kiss. I feel her body melting into mine.

"Make love to me, Preston," she whispers against my lips. "Please."

Pulling back, I stare at her. She looks so broken, so vulnerable right now. I'd love nothing more than to sink myself balls deep inside of her, but at the same time, I want to know what's upset her so much.

"I will, on one condition."

"Anything," she says.

"After you need to tell me why you were a blubbering mess on my doorstep just now."

She swallows deeply and then nods. Standing up, she unbuttons her shirt slowly. Then she pushes the linen off her shoulders and the material flutters to the floor. She reaches behind her back to unclasp her bra. The straps fall down her arms, baring her breasts to me. Her gorgeous plump breasts. "You have the most gorgeous breasts, Cress."

She straddles my thighs and stares intently at me. The light in her eyes is returning. Leaning forward, I suck a nipple into my mouth. "Preston," she moans, her head dropping back as I lick, suck, and bite her breasts. She runs her fingers up the back of my neck, gently tugging on my hair. My cock thickens beneath us.

Cress grips my cheeks. "Make love to me, Preston."

Who am I to deny her? I stand up with her in my arms and walk into the bedroom. Placing her on her feet, we stare at each other as we undress. Our eyes are locked on one another, the air in the room thick with desire. We are both naked and panting. Stepping to her, I slide my hands around her waist and press my lips to hers. She drapes her arms around my shoulders and kisses me back. It's soft, it's sensual, it's the definition of a perfect kiss.

Spinning her around, I lay her back on the bed. Staring down at her, I have never seen a more stunning vision. Her hair is fanned beneath her, creating a golden blonde halo. Against the darkness of my comforter it looks like it's glowing.

"You are magnificent, Cress," I say, nudging her legs open with my knee. I cover her body with mine. My cock is at her entrance, she pleads with her eyes for me to push inside of her and I do exactly that. Her walls hug my cock as I slide in and out. I stare down at her as I thrust my hips back and forth. Our eyes are locked on one another; nothing else exists right now except Cress and me. She lifts her leg, hooking it around my lower back, allowing me to thrust deeper. I can feel my balls tingling but I will myself not to come before her, she needs too and right now because I don't know how much longer I can last.

"Come with me," she moans. She reaches up and cups my cheek in her palm, that one action means everything to me. She clenches around me and screams, this causes me to explode with her.

Together we ride out our orgasm. I somehow feel closer to her in this moment. Her hand is still cupping my cheek, she runs her finger along my jawline. She stares intently up at me and murmurs, "I love you, Preston."

I look down at her and smile. "I love you too, Cress."

We gaze at one another, our love enveloping us. She slides her hand behind my head and pulls me down to kiss her. Our tongues gently caress one another, sliding in and out of our mouths. My cock hardens as we continue to kiss, I know Cress can feel it because she smiles into our kiss. She flips me onto my back and rests her hands on my chest, lifting to her knees she slides herself down my cock. Our eyes are glued together as she rides my cock. Lifting my hands, I caress her breasts. Rolling her nipples between my thumbs and forefingers. Her head drops back, and she slides her hands into her hair in that sexy way. She flicks her hair up, the strands dropping back down; never have I seen anything more sexy than a naked Cress riding my cock.

"Come for me, Cress," I say, as I press my thumb to her clit.

This sets her off and she moans my name as she comes for a second time. She clenches down on me and I too come.

She collapses onto my chest. I hug her to me, running

my hand up and down her back. She lifts her gaze to mine. "I really do love you, Preston."

"And I really do love you too, Cress."

She lowers her head back to my chest and sighs deeply. She knows that we need to talk. I don't want to push her but it's killing me not knowing why she was so upset earlier. "I met Creed my last year at college." She hugs me tighter and continues, "I saw him in the local coffee shop. He looked across the room at me and our eyes met, it was lust at first sight. We fell hard and fast for each other. After graduation, we moved in together. Life was great. I had a teaching job at the same school as Ave, I had a great boyfriend, everything was prefect but it slowly started to fall apart. Creed changed, I don't know exactly when it happened, but he started to become nasty, saying horrible things to me. He'd always apologize and things would go back to normal. When I found out I was pregnant, I was over the moon...until Creed came home. He wasn't happy and told me to get rid of it. He also accused me of cheating and that it probably wasn't even his. He left but came home a few hours later all apologetic. I accepted his apology and things were good. For a little while anyway. It all went to shit when I was twenty weeks, he missed the scan and when I got home, he was packing. He said some really horrible things and walked out. I was pregnant, alone, and heartbroken." She lifts her head and sadly smiles at me.

"Cress," I say, brushing her hair off her face. "You really are remarkable. That must have been really hard to go through."

"It was. Thankfully I had Mom and Ave, those two were my everything, until I gave birth to Lexi that is. She became my whole world the moment I laid eyes on her."

"What happened after she was born with *him*?" I place emphasis on the word him.

"Much to Mom and Ave's disgust, I reached out to let him know he had a daughter. No surprises he didn't give two shits, that was until I bumped into his mom one day at the store. When I told her what happened she was so angry with her son. After that he made an effort but as time went on, he drifted away. I'll never stop him seeing his daughter, I see that too much at school. That just hurts the child. Just because I have an issue with Creed, Lexi shouldn't miss out on seeing her dad. Even if I do think he's a big dick."

"More people need to be like you in situations like this." I pause. "So what happened today?"

She sighs and closes her eyes. She hops up and starts to pace. My eyes watch her walk back and forth. She swallows deeply, stops, and stares at me. "Over the years, I've had weak moments and I'd give in to Creed and his charm. I'd sleep with him and deep down, I always hoped that he'd stay and we'd become a happy family. I realized that was never going to happen so a few months back, I decided it wasn't healthy for me to keep going back to him. I told myself that I'd stop sleeping with him. He doesn't like being told no, and for the last few weeks his anger at being told no has been building. The verbal attacks have been getting worse, and I'm pretty sure he's bad-mouthing me to Lexi too."

"Is that why he shoved you the other week?"

She nods, her eyes full of tears. "He's slowly unravelling, Preston. He's slapped me before but he's never been violent. I'm almost scared to let Lexi spend time with him, but I'm scared of what he'll do to me if I stop him from spending time with her. Deep down I know he won't hurt Lex—"

"Are you sure about that?"

She looks to me as the first tear falls. She shakes her head and wipes it away. "I really don't know." She cries, the tears are now pouring down her cheeks.

Hopping off the bed, I stand up, wrap her in my arms and let her cry. I whisper, "Shhhh," over and over to her, consoling the woman I love as she lets out all her grief concerning Creed-fucking-Dawson.

"Preston," she sniffles into my chest, "what am I going to do?" I hold her tighter to me and place a kiss on her head. She is literally shaking with fear., My heart hurts for her.

"We will get through this together, Cress. I won't let anything happen to you or Lexi." I press another kiss to her head as I say this.

Shaking her head, she lifts her head and looks up at me. "I can't ask that of you."

"You're not asking, I'm offering." We silently stare at one another, she processes what I just said. A smile graces her face.

"Thank you," she sadly says, she seems so broken right now.

I need to take her out and keep her mind off this. We can come up with a game plan later. "Okay, you need to go take a shower and then I'm taking you out for coffee and cake. Then we will pick something up for dinner and be waiting at your place for when Princess Lexi and douche dad get home—"

"His nickname is Dickwad Dawson."

"I like that." I place a kiss on her nose. "Now go shower, you stink like sex."

"I wonder why that would be?" she teases.

"Well, when a penis enters a vagina over and over again, that's called sex."

"Guarantee what we did has a much better description than that."

"I was paraphrasing," I nonchalantly say. "Now shower." I turn her around, tap her ass, and push her toward the shower.

She looks over her shoulder at me. "You can always join me."

"Cress, if I join you in the shower, there is no way I won't fuck you again and next time I do, I want to take my time and show you how much I love you."

She stares at me, processing my words. "Fine," she huffs. "I have fingers, looks like I'll just have to look after myself."

"Can I watch?"

"Why, Dr. Knight, I didn't realize you were a voyeur."

"When it comes to you, Cressida Bayliss, I will voy like no-one has ever voyed before."

"You say such the sweetest things but if you ever call me Cressida again, you'll be getting reacquainted with Mrs. Palmer and her five daughters." She blows me a kiss, turns around, and walks into the en suite and turns the shower on.

Sitting on the edge of my bed, I process her words. Creed Dawson is a real piece of work and I meant what I said earlier, I won't let anything happen to her or Lexi.

18 CRESS

It's been a week since my mini meltdown and a week of radio silence from Creed. He wasn't impressed that Preston was here when he dropped Lex home after the circus. I think he had it in his head that giving me a few hours of 'me' time would result in me wanting to jump his bones. That will never happen again. The Creed train has left the station, and Cress is happily on board the Preston Express, not that there is anything express about this man. Even a quickie with him is anything but quick. My mind drifts to the day after my meltdown…

…Preston pops around after his shift. Lexi's eye light up when she opens the door and sees him. I think it was more to do with the bunch of lollipops for her rather than him. She lets him in and they both join me in the kitchen. He places a kiss on my cheek and winks, my body instantly buzzing from just a kiss. He must sense my reaction because he mouths 'later' to me.

He opens a lollipop for Lexi and hands it to her. "Yuck," she says, dumping it into my coffee cup.

"Lexi," I scoff.

"It was a green one, Mommy, that's yucky."

Shaking my head, I pull it out of my cup and pop it into my mouth. Preston opens a purple one and hands it to her. "Thank you, Prince Dr. Preston."

"You are welcome, Princess Lexi. How about you go watch some Pony before I take my two ladies out for an early dinner?"

"Really?" she excitedly asks.

"Of course."

She races out of the kitchen into the living room, a few minutes later the theme song to Pony starts. Preston stalks over to me, pulls the lollipop from my mouth, grips my cheeks, and kisses me.

"Well, hello to you too," I say, taking the lollipop from him and popping it back into my mouth.

He has a carnal look in his eyes, he leans forward and whispers, "Cress, I am going to feast on your pussy and you are going to remain quiet. You make a peep and I stop. Nod if you agree."

My head nods, as if I'd say no to that.

He places his hands on my shoulders and pushes me into the corner farthest from the living room. Dropping to his knees, he pushes my dress up my legs. His touch sets my body ablaze. He kisses my clit through the material of my panties, which are completely soaked. He slides them down my legs and I step out, kicking them to the side. I lean back against the counter, pushing my pussy into his face. With his eyes locked on mine, he grips my hips in his hands and licks me from taint to clit.

A moan escapes my lips. "Cress," he warns before he thrusts his tongue back into me.

Gripping the edge of the counter, I close my eyes and give myself over to him. I'm panting as my orgasm builds. He pulls back suddenly, leaving me unsatisfied. Reaching up, he takes the lollipop from my mouth and pops it into his mouth. He sucks it before tracing the candy around my clit. My eyes widen when he slides the sucker between my lips. "Ohh God!" I pant, as he pushes it inside of me. Biting my lip, I hold back a moan as he continues to push it in and out of me.

He sucks and nibbles on my clit as he vigorously pumps the candy in and out of me. His eyes are locked on mine as the pleasure within me grows.

"Come for me, Cress," he whispers against my sensitive bud, his words set me off and I come all over his face and the lollipop.

He pops the sucker into his mouth and sucks. "Fuck, Cress. Your taste is so much sweeter mixed with this lollipop, a Cress pop is my few fav candy."

He rises up, leans his hands on the counter either side of me, cocooning me in. We stare at one another, I'm still panting from my quick and intense orgasm. Reaching out I squeeze his cock. "Maybe I should—"

"Mooommy," Lexi yells, "I need to go poo poo." He rests his forehead against mine and we both laugh. "Mooooomm," she yells again.

"You head to the toilet and I'll be in in a sec."

"Okay," she yells back, and we hear her race down the hallway.

Taking the lollipop from him, I pop it into my mouth and wink. Dropping down, I grab my panties and pull them back on before going to deal with Lexi and her ill-timed poop...

I'm snapped back to the present when Lexi yells out, "Moooooom, I need to go poo poo." A laugh escapes me, it's like time repeating itself.

"Coming," I yell.

Lexi and I are snuggling on the sofa, watching *Frozen 2*. My mind is not on the movie, I keep thinking about Preston. I don't think I have ever been happier than I am right now. Preston came into my life at the exact moment I needed him. If it weren't for him, I don't think I would have survived Creed's taunts over the last few weeks.

I love him with all my heart. Not only does he love me but he loves Lexi as if she were his own. Seeing the two of them together absolutely melts my heart. Who would have thought my best friend and I would both be blissfully in love at the same time? And with best friends too? When I think about Ave, I smile and as if she can sense me thinking about her, my phone rings and I'm met with her smiling face.

"Hey, Ave."

"Hey, yourself. It feels like forever since we've spoken."

"I know, right? But someone is all loved up and I have been trumped as your person."

"You will always be my person, Cress, but Flynn has a dick and you don't."

"Avery Evans, I have never heard you speak like that before. I wholehcartedly approve of you finally joining the Crass Cress club."

"I wouldn't go that far. Anyway, what's new with you?"

"Creed's a dick."

"That's not new. What did Dickwad do now?"

"Got mad when I wouldn't sleep with him."

"You turned down sex? Are you sick? Or is there something you're hiding?"

That's when it hits me, I haven't spoken to Ave about

Preston. Actually, I haven't seen her since she hooked up with Flynn.

"How about we meet for drinks on Friday night, and we can catch up on the gossip?"

"I would love that, Ave. Message me when you're in the Uber on your way to Mom's."

"It's a date...and I want all the gossip."

"Same goes for you."

"Deal."

We say our goodbyes and then I call Mom and lock in a sleepover for Lexi. As predicted, she was happy to have her granddaughter for the night.

Life is perfect at the moment and I cannot wait to let loose with my bestie tomorrow night.

Lexi and I spend the day pampering each other. Me getting ready for my night out with Ave, and Lexi because she really believes she's a princess at the moment.

After getting dressed—me in jeans and a sparkly top, and Lexi, in the princess dress Preston bought her—we jump into my car and head over to Mom's. As we are pulling out of the driveway, I notice a gray sedan on the other side of the street. I've never seen it before, it pulls away and I shake off the weird feeling.

Just as I pull up at Mom's, my phone pings with a text. After hustling Lexi inside, I check my message.

AVERY: *In Uber now...let's get our drink on*
CRESS: *See you soon **cocktail emoji times 3***

Mom tells me I can pick Lexi up anytime and for me to have a great time. A car horn beeps. "That'll be Ave." I walk over to Lexi, "You be good for Nanna, I'll pick you up tomorrow."

"Love you, Mommy." She hugs me and sits next to Mom on the sofa.

"Have fun," Mom says, as I walk out to the Uber.

Climbing in next to Ave, I smile. "Hey hey, babycakes."

"Babycakes, really?"

"Yeah, not one of my finer greetings but the night is young, I have all night to come up with some awesome one-liners."

Forty minutes later, we pull up at the Fat Fox. Walking inside, we head to the bar and excitement bubbles in the both of us when we see the cocktail of the day is a mojito. "Winning," I say, as I order two. Ave waits for our drinks and I go grab the table recently vacated by a couple.

A few minutes later, Ave arrives with our drinks. She hands one to me and we raise our glasses. "Cheers," we say in unison. We clink our glasses together and drink. I moan as the tart, tangy liquid quenches my thirst; I take another sip when her phone begins to ring. Her face lights up and one guess who it is. "It's Flynn," she says, "give me a sec."

Nodding at her, I realize that my drink is nearly empty. Chugging back what was left, I point to the bar and mimic drinking. Ave nods at me and I make my way to the bar to order more drinks. It takes what feels like forever to get our new drinks, as I return to the table, Ave says, "I love you," and hangs up, just as I place our new drinks on the table.

"You only love me for my cocktails," I tease.

"Yeah, and?" she sasses back in reply. She picks up her

new drink and raises it up for a toast. "To a fantabulous night with my fabulous girlfriend."

"Cheers to that."

We both sip and let out an, "ahh," as the refreshing drink dances on our taste buds.

"What's got you so chipper?" I ask, my body swaying to the music.

"Flynn and Preston are stopping by. I hope that's okay?"

My eyes widen in delight, as much as I was looking forward to girls' night, I've been missing Preston this week. I realize I haven't answered her and from the look in her eyes, she's about to grill me for information so I quickly say, "Is it okay that two sexy as sin doctors want to stop by? One who happens to have a sexy as hell Irish accent, and the other could be Channing Tatum's twin, let me think about that...hell to the yes it's okay." Taking another sip, I moan, *Man, this is a good mojito.*

Looking to Ave, I sigh, "I'm gonna get laid tonight."

"Get Cress laid is my mission tonight." Ave states but little does she know, I'll be going home with Preston. I'm not sure why I'm not telling her about him. I kinda like the mystery of it and I haven't felt this way about a guy since Creed. This is all new and exciting for me.

"I like this sassy side of you, Ave. Who knew you getting laid would also be good for me too? Prior to Flynn, you'd never suggest something like that."

"I know, right? I'm just so happy and I want you to be happy too." *I am happy,* I think to myself.

"Ahh, thanks, babe, but try not get finger fucked here again, save that for the privacy of home, or at the least, the car."

She chokes on her drink and shakes her head at me. "Why did I tell you that?"

"Because you know I need to fuck vicariously through you at the moment. My rabbit died from overuse, and at the rate I'm going my bullet is going to burn a hole in my clit."

"Evening, ladies," Preston says from behind me, my eyes bug wide open at what he just heard. My cheeks darken with embarrassment, while my best friend, possible ex-best friend just laughs at me.

Tonight is off to a swimming start and I cannot wait to see how the rest of the evening progresses now that Flynn and Preston are here.

19 PRESTON

As soon as Flynn and I enter The Fat Fox, I immediately spot the girls. My eyes always gravitate to Cress whenever she's in the room. Flynn leads us over to the girls and when we arrive, I hear Cress talking about a vibrator. "Evening, ladies," I say, startling Cress and causing Avery to laugh. She immediately stops laughing when she sees Flynn. The two of them make out like lovesick teenagers. I can't help but tease them, "Get a fuckin' room, you two."

Flynn places Avery back on her feet, she winks at me as I take a seat. I watch the two of them and I realize, she really is the perfect person for my best friend. Sure they are total opposites but as the saying goes, opposites attract.

"Preston, great to see you again," Ave says sweetly.

"You too, Avery." I turn my attention over to Cress, who's quiet for a change. "Cressida," I tease, "it's nice to make your acquaintance again." I play that we don't know each other because we haven't had 'that' chat yet. From the look on her face, she seems anxious to play coy so I continue, "I'm Preston Knight, pediatric doctor and this thing's best friend." Our eyes are locked on one another, she looks fucking amazing tonight and I cannot help but admire her beauty. Even in jeans and a simple top, Cress is the sexiest woman in the place.

"Thing, really?" Flynn scoffs. I just shrug my shoulders and continue to focus on Cress.

"Cressida Bayliss, but my friends call me Cress," she purrs in reply. "I'm a mom and this sex fiend's bestie." She nods her head at Avery and takes a sip from her drink.

"And are we a sex fiend too?" I question her, eager to hear her reply because I know the answer, and it's a resounding yes.

She nonchalantly shrugs her shoulders and takes another sip of her drink, seductively wrapping her lips around the straw. After taking a drink, she quietly murmurs, "You already know the answer to that..." and then adds, "...and you may find out again later."

"Are you offering horizontal tango lessons?"

"Maybe," she coos, as she takes another sip of her cocktail.

Watching her wrap her lips around the straw, my cock hardens. 'Minx,' I mouth to her and then I notice Flynn and Avery eye fucking the hell out of one another. We are not even a blip on their radar right now.

"They're eye fucking each other again."

Cress replies with, "At least he isn't finger fucking her."

Ave's mouth drops open in shock. "Cress," she scolds.

"Crass Cress strikes again," I say, this causes Avery to

burst out laughing. Looking to her, I scrunch my eyes. "What?"

"That was this one here's," she flicks her thumb to Cress, "nickname in school."

"Yet you still love me, crassness and all," Cress says to Ave.

"Well, I'm not telling you anything any more. You'll have to suffice with your bullet from now on."

Leaning into her, I not so quietly whisper, "I'm more than happy to assist you."

Flynn and Ave look on in confusion, I'm pretty sure they know something is going on between Cress and me, but being the good friends they are, they don't push the issue.

We stay at the tavern for a few hours before we decide to move on to this new club, Tingle, that my brother, Keeton, told me about. When we arrive, we head straight to the bar. We do a round of tequila shots before we snag a table by the dance floor.

Looking out at the dance floor, I notice a girl with vibrant copper orange hair, then I notice my brother, and his business partner, Blair, dancing with her. In a throuple. My brother leads a double life. In the office he's all professional and business-like, but behind closed doors, he's a kinky fucking bastard. I watch the three of them, they are pretty hot together, then I realize I'm watching my brother get down and dirty on the dance floor. Shaking my head, I turn my attention back to Cress. Her eyes are glazed, she's on her way to drunk town; we all are actually. "Acceptable in the 80's" by Calvin Harris begins playing. Flynn and I look to one another, and we surprise Cress and Ave when we jump up and make our way to the edge of the dance floor. Flynn and I start to dance, and just like in college, we get down and dirty. My inner dancer slash stripper comes out to play. Flynn and I bump and grind away to the beat of the music. Our moves draw in a crowd, everyone mesmerized by the two of us. They cheer and egg us on. The song changes to one I don't know, I look to Flynn and he nods, so we walk back over to the girls.

"Holy shit, dudes, where did you guys learn to dance like that?" Cress asks, as she hands us each a beer.

"Med school," we reply in unison.

"Preston and I were the dance kings in our frat house." Flynn says, draping his arm along the back of Ave's chair.

"You guys were in a frat?" Cress and Ave both ask at the same time.

"Jinx," Cress says. Ave shrugs and turns her attention to Flynn, waiting for his reply.

"Yeah," he nods, "Preston and I were Phi Kappa Psi at Stanford."

"I did not pick you as a frat guy."

Flynn and Avery are flirting in that sickly way, so I look to Cress. "Would you like to dance?" As I ask that, my mind drifts to our first date and the dance, in both the restaurant and once we got back to my place.

"I'd love to." She places her hand in mine and stands up. Lacing my fingers with hers, I escort her to the dance floor. Spinning her around, I pull her into me. She wraps her arm around me and I'm transported back to the naked sexy dance she did for me on our first date, followed by my naked horizontal tango lesson.

A few songs later, Flynn and Avery join us. "Sexy Back" by JT starts to play. We all bump and grind and we take each other on in a dance-off. Somehow it becomes Cress and Ave against Flynn and me, but we totally kick their asses. We left Cress and Ave for dead, but watching

Cress grind against Ave is hot. I'm not into the threesome thing like my brother, but I can appreciate two chicks grinding against each other. And when one of those chicks is Cress, it's hotter than hot.

The rest of the night flies by. We slam back shots like we are in college again and then we dance some more. As the night wears on, Cress and I dance dirtier and dirtier. It probably isn't appropriate when in public but when you're in a club named Tingle, I think it's fair game.

At stupid o'clock in the morning, Flynn and Ave say their goodbyes. They can hardly keep their hands off one another. Cress and I stay at the club for a little while longer. Our dances are becoming more and more erotic, they are borderline not suitable for public. I'm glad Cress is in jeans because if she wasn't, who knows what I would have done.

"Let's get out of here," I whisper into her ear, as her body shivers against mine.

She nods her head. I order us an Uber and link my fingers with hers. When we make our way outside, the cool night air slaps us in the face. Cress shivers, I drop her hand and pull her to me, my front to her back. She rubs her ass against my cock. "Cress," I warn, "you need to stop that or I'm going to drag you into the alleyway over there, pull your jeans down and fuck you."

"I'm down with that," she sasses back.

Clearly sexual threats don't work with her but luckily for me, our Uber pulls up. We climb in and I reconfirm my address with the driver. Surprisingly, Cress behaves on the trip back to my place, but as soon as I unlock the front door, she turns into the sexual deviant I love. We don't make it past the entryway before I'm balls deep inside her.

This woman will be the death of me, but death by Cress would be a wonderful way to go.

Eventually we make it to bed. We fall asleep naked and happily wrapped in each other's embrace…not knowing that in the coming weeks, things will change in a way that no one sees coming.

20 CRESS

WAKING THE NEXT MORNING, I FEEL LIKE SHIT. I'M TOO OLD to party the night away like I did—I'm not twenty-one anymore—but man it was fun. My body hurts and I don't know if it's from all the dancing or the mind-blowing sex when we got home. I cannot remember the last time I had a night like that.

Reaching over, I'm met with a cold sheet. Opening my eyes, I notice I'm alone in bed. Sitting up, I hear splashing from outside. Climbing out of bed, I head out to the pool area. Leaning on the pool gate, I watch as Preston does lap after lap. He swims up and down, flipping around and swimming back. His body cuts through the water like a hot knife in butter; smooth and with ease. His muscles stretching and flexing with each stroke. He reaches the end, stops, and stands up; his back is to me. His muscles taut as he runs his hands through his hair, removing the excess water.

"Morning." I say, startling him, as I open the gate and step into the pool area.

He turns to face me and when he notices I'm still naked, his eyes fill with heat. "Good morning, Love." His eyes roam over my body, my skin heats even though I'm at the opposite end of the pool from him. He beckons me forward with this finger.

Shaking my head, I purse my lips and take a seat on the edge of the pool. My legs dangle in the water, it's colder than I anticipated and my body breaks out in goose-bumps. With my eyes on his, I trace my finger down my neck, across the tops of my breasts. I circle my nipples before tracing down my stomach, spreading my legs open. He stalks toward me as I run the tip of my finger up and down my folds. He stops in front of me and places his hand on top of mine. He takes control. Pressing his hand to mine, as he slips our fingers between my lips. Sliding them up and down, he presses into me, only to pull back and slide them back up toward my clit.

"Please," I moan. My body is on fire. Every nerve ending alive and buzzing.

"This is *my* pussy, Cress. You need to remember that."

Before I can agree, he pushes my hand aside and thrusts two fingers into me. Spreading my legs wider, he lowers his head and sucks my clit into his mouth. If I thought I was on fire before, I'm now a fiery inferno. Every fiber within engulfed with desire and lust. He slips a finger into my ass and I explode.

"Prestooooonn," I mewl, falling backward as the most intense orgasm of my life detonates. Lifting my hands, I squeeze my breasts and clench my legs around his head as he continues to suck my clit and pump his fingers in and out of both my pussy and ass. The orgasm that never ends continues to erupt and I ride it out.

Lying on the edge of the pool, I'm breathing deeply, coming down from my orgasmic high. My body is still buzzing when I sit up and stare at Preston. He has a satisfied smirk on his face. "Don't look so smug, Dr. Knight, you haven't got off yet."

"Cress, giving you pleasure gives me pleasure. Now come here and kiss me."

Sliding into the water, I shiver when the cool water hits my heated skin. Swimming over to Preston, I place my arms around his neck and pull him toward me. Our lips press together, I lick along his seam, slipping my tongue into his mouth. He slides his hands down my body and lifts me up, I wrap my legs around his waist. His cock is harder than steel, circling my hips on his cock he groans into my mouth. He walks us back until I'm pressed up against the pool wall, pushing himself inside. My head drops back and I meet him thrust for thrust. Even though I just had an intense orgasm, my body begins to thrum once again.

Lifting my head, I stare into his green orbs and I give myself over to him. Our bodies rock back and forth. The pleasure builds and builds. "Let go, Love," Preston croons and I do exactly that, the pleasure envelops me and for the second time this morning I reach my climax. Moaning into his mouth, I ride out my orgasm. Soon after, his body stills and he too comes.

We stay wrapped in each other's embrace as our breathing returns to normal.

"I love you," I whisper, as I continue to stare at him.

"I love you too, Cress. You are everything I didn't

realize I was missing. Both you and Lexi mean everything to me."

My heart melts at his words, cupping his cheek in my palm. I smile, "You mean everything to us too. We are lucky to have met you." It's crazy to be feeling like this after such a short amount of time, but when you know, you know. I'd be crazy to let a man like Preston go. I will do everything I can to keep him because I'm happier than I've ever been before.

"How about we go pick her up and take her to the park for a picnic?"

"She'd love that…and I would too."

He kisses the tip of my nose and lifts me up, placing me on the edge of the pool. He lifts himself up beside me. We sit with our legs in the pool, I rest my head on his shoulder. The moment is perfect, absolutely perfect.

We head inside to shower before we pick Lexi up and my phone pings, I deviate to my purse on the hall table. "I'll get this and meet you in there."

"Don't be long," he says, and I watch his naked ass walk away from me.

Picking up my phone, I deflate when I see the messages are from Creed. They started an hour ago and there are quite a few of them.

CREED: *Where the fuck are you?*

CREED: *Answer me, bitch*

CREED: *If you don't answer me, I will make your life a living hell*

CREED: *Where the fuck are you?*

CREED: *Cressida fucking Bayliss*

CREED: *Fucking tell me where are you!*

My heart rate speeds up as I read through the messages when my phone rings in my hand. I cringe when I see it's Creed calling. I know that if I don't answer, he'll just keep harassing me. Taking a deep breath, I answer.

"Hello," I say, my voice strong.

"Where the fuck are you?" he snarls.

"Hello to you too, Creed," I sass back.

"Don't fuck with me, bitch, where are you and Baby Girl?"

"We're out, and her name is Lexi, not Baby Girl, it's creepy when a grown man refers to a child like that."

"I can call her squid or Baby Girl, or Kid like you call her Munchkin."

"You don't have the right to use a nickname with her. Her. Name. Is. Lexi."

"Get fucked, now, where are you?"

"Out," I snap back, anger coursing through my veins right now.

"I can see that, I'm at your house."

"We won't be home 'til later, you are more than welcome to stop by then...or tomorrow." *Or never*, I silently add.

"Of course I'm welcome, I can stop by whenever the fuck I want. You need to start remembering your place, Cressida. Don't make me angry. You will regret it if you do. You wouldn't want something to happen to Baby Girl now, would you?"

"Don't you threaten my daughter, Creed." I snarl, thorough clench teeth. "You—"

"I can say, threaten, and do whatever the fuck I want."

He hangs up before I can reply, my eyes well with angry tears but I refuse to cry another single tear over this man. Shaking my head, I close my eyes and take a deep breath. I'm so lost in my head; I don't hear Preston come back into the room. "Cress, Love, what's wrong?"

Lifting my head up, I look to Preston. I open and close my mouth a few times, no words come out and then my brain finally fires. "Just Creed being Creed," I tell him but he knows I'm hiding something. I won't let Creed get to me and ruin what has been an amazing night and morning. If I do, he wins and he doesn't deserve to win. I won't allow him to win.

"How about that shower?" I say, as I walk past him and head into the en suite. Turning the shower on, I step in, close my eyes, and let the water wash away all my worries.

Opening my eyes, I see Preston staring at me through the door. His gaze calms me, I know with him on my side, I'll be fine. He will give me the strength I need to stand up to Creed...I hope.

21 CRESS

THE FOLLOWING SATURDAY IS A BEAUTIFUL CLEAR DAY SO Mom and I take Lexi to Navy Pier. Preston is working all weekend which sucks, but I get to spend time with my daughter and mom, so it's still a win. We pack a bag and I make sure to pack her inhaler just in case her asthma kicks up from running around and all the excitement. Last time we went, I didn't have it on me and she had an attack. I won't be making that rookie mistake again.

As usual, I get more texts from Creed, and they all ask the same two things, 'Where the fuck are you?' and 'Ready to fuck yet?' Ummm, no, hell will freeze over before that happens again. Even if Preston wasn't in the picture, that ship has sailed. It's left port, never to return again. Creed and I are officially done in that respect. Unfortunately, he's Lexi's father so he still has to be a part of our lives.

It's really busy here today, people are obviously lapping up the warmer weather. We have just gotten off the Ferris wheel and Lexi is beaming. She's jumping up and down all excited when she steps into the path of a kid on a scooter. The two of them collide and it's nasty.

My poor lil' munchkin gets hit and knocked down, with the kid and his scooter landing on top of her. She screams out and begins to cry. "Lexi!" I scream, as I race over to her. "Why didn't you stop? Or go around her? She's only a kid."

"I'm so sorry," the teenage boy says, as he rolls off Lexi, pushing his scooter to the side, he looks down at her. "Are you okay?"

"Of course she's not," I shout, "you just crushed her with your scooter. There's blood everywhere.

One of the friends says, "Ohhhhhhh shit, Dustin's gonna get it."

"It's okay," Mom placates, "it was an accident." Trying to calm the situation.

"Mom, she's bleeding and a kid was just on top of her. It's anything but fine," I snap at Mom.

"Where is she hurt?" the boy asks, he's worried and I don't know if it's for Lexi, or his own ass.

"Lexi, baby, look at Mommy."

Lexi is wailing and crying. Tears stain her little cheeks, she has a gash on her arm and leg. She's covered in blood. She must be in a lot of pain. The boy who hit her rips off his shirt and presses it to Lexi's arm. "Brent, gimme your shirt for her leg." The friend peels off his shirt and presses it to her leg.

"What are you doing?" I ask, watching as they both spring into action and tend to Lexi.

"We just did first aid at school, we're putting our training into action."

Dammit, I can't yell now. They are actually helping, I can feel Lexi start to calm down. She flinches each time they hold their shirts to her body but her tears are subsiding. "Well, you are both doing a great job."

"Lexi, baby, look at Mommy, don't look at the blood. Focus on me and my voice."

"Moooommmy, I bleeding," she cries.

"I know, Munchkin, I think we will have to stop by the hospital."

"I want Prince Dr. Knight."

"I will see if I can arrange that, but he might be busy."

Mom takes over looking after Lexi while I pull out my phone and call Preston. It goes straight to voicemail, I leave a message but I also text him.

CRESS: *Lexi had an accident, on our way to the ER. Please come if you can*

Putting my phone into my pocket, I bend down and pick Lexi up. "Nanna and I will take you to the hospital now." Looking to Dustin and Brent, I smile at them. "Thank you for your help. I'm sorry she jumped in front of you."

"It's okay," the boy who hit her says, "she reminds me of my little sister, Alexis."

"That's my fullded name," Lexi tells the boy.

"Well, if you are like my sister then I know you'll be fine. She's tough, it must go with the name."

"I'm tough AND a princess."

"Wow, that's a double whammy right there. I have no doubt you will be fine then, Princess Lexi."

"Mommy, he called me princess."

"Thank you again, Dustin," I say. "And sorry for yelling at you."

"It's okay, I'm sorry, too. I should have been more careful."

Turning around, with Lexi in my arms, Mom and I race to the car and head to the hospital. Mom drives and I'm in the back with Lex. My phone pings with a text and I pull it out.

PRESTON: *I'm in the ER, see you when you get here. Give my princess a kiss for me*
CRESS: *Will do. See you soon*

"That was Preston, he's waiting at the ER for you."

Lexi nods at me. Her tears have stopped, that's a relief. "How you doing, Munchkin?"

"My leg really hurts, Mommy."

"I know, baby. Preston will make you all better." Looking up, I see Mom pulling into the hospital grounds. "We're here," I say and just as I say that, the car door swings open. Preston is standing there staring down at us.

"Princess Lexi, what happened?"

"I got hurtded," she says, lifting her arm and leg to him, wincing as she moves in my arms.

"Well, let's get you inside and all cleaned up."

Shuffling across the seat toward the open door, I pop one leg on the ground but Preston bends down and takes her from my arms. She cries out in pain and it breaks my heart. Seeing your baby hurt is the worst feeling in the world, but I know Preston will look after her.

Following them inside, we head toward a cubicle where an older nurse is waiting for us. "Okay, Princess," Preston says to Lexi, his voice soft and caring, "I'm going to pop you on the bed here and have a look at you." Lexi nods her head. "And Mom," he looks to me and with that one glance, I know Lexi and I are in good hands...I may also be a little turned on seeing him all alpha doctor like, but now isn't the time for that, "how about you sit on the other side and hold this brave princess's hand." Nodding my head, I do as I'm told.

The nurse squeezes my shoulder. "She's in good hands, Dr. Knight is the best."

"He sure is," Lexi says. "He bought me a crown."

The nurse nods. "Ahh, you must be *the* Lexi we've all heard so much about." She looks to me. "And you must be Cress." The look she gives me is like that of a proud mom, beaming over her son.

"That's us," I say.

"I'm Andi, Preston's number one nurse. Your munchkin really is in good hands, and I'm not just saying that because of who you are to him, I'm saying that because he really is the best."

Nodding my head, I process her words. I'm shocked that someone from his work knows who we are but at the same time, my heart fills with joy that he's talking about us with his work colleagues. But if they know, I'm guessing Flynn will know and that means Avery will know...but if she knew, she'd call me to tell me she knew and she'd be pressing me to get all the gossip. Therefore, I don't think she knows, but now I'm wondering if she does know and she just hasn't said anything because she's waiting for me to let her know. I really need to arrange a coffee date, or cocktails so I can fill her in on all things Preston and me because I'm rambling to myself right now and I don't ramble, that's Ave's job.

Lexi cries out when Preston pours something over the cut on her leg. She has my attention now. Taking her hand in mine, I coo, "Shhhh, Munchkin, you are big and brave. You'll be okay."

"Right you are, Lexi," Preston says. "I just need to clean this and then we can pop a bandage on it." He looks to me, "No need for stitches which is good."

"Okay," she nods, "can I have a pink bandage?"

"I have something better in mind, after I dress it, how about I pop a *My Little Pony* Band-Aid on it and if we sweet talk Andi, I'm sure she will give you a couple to take home too."

"Really?" Lexi says, her voice laced with excitement.

"Only the best for my most fav patient."

Thirty minutes later, Lexi is all bandaged up—surprisingly, neither one needed stitches—and we are now on our way home.

We say goodbye to Preston and Andi, I don't get a chance to ask if he's able to come over later after his shift because he's whisked away on another case.

Traffic is terrible this afternoon and it takes us forever to get home. We stop at McDonald's and get Lex a happy meal for dinner. She eats most of it. Mom tidies up and I bathe her and get her ready for bed. Lexi is wiped out and as soon as her little head hits the pillow, she's out cold.

Sitting beside her, I stare and watch her sleep, she's my everything. I love her with all my heart. I always have, and I always will until my dying breath.

Kissing her on the forehead, I walk back into the living room and smile when I see Preston sitting with Mom on the sofa. A bottle of red is open and he's telling her about med school and being a doctor. Leaning against the wall, I watch as he and Mom chat. Creed never did this, it was always about him.

He looks over his shoulder and smiles at me. "She asleep?"

Nodding my head, I walk over to him. "Yeah, I think she was asleep before her head hit the pillow." Kissing him on the cheek, I snuggle in next to him. The next thing, I know, I'm in bed, snuggled next to Preston.

His alarm goes off at stupid o'clock; he kisses me on the forehead and leaves for work. I drift back to sleep but I toss and turn. I wake with a fright from a horrible nightmare: Creed took Lexi. I was spinning around in a crowd, screaming for her, but everyone just went about their business as if my worst fear hadn't happened.

After that, I can't sleep. Deciding to hop up, I head out to the kitchen and notice Mom asleep on the sofa. Grabbing the blanket from the back of the armchair, I cover her and step into the kitchen to make a coffee. With my cup in hand, I sit at the island and think about my dream.

"What's wrong?" Mom asks, as she grabs a mug and makes herself a coffee.

"Bad dream."

"Lexi's fine, Cress. You need to stop worrying."

"I'm her mom, it's my job to worry."

Over the next week, that dream plagues me each night; it's worrying because Creed has stopped texting and stopping by. It's radio silent from him. Preston on the other hand, has stopped by each day to check on Lexi and me. And I blissfully fall asleep in his arms…until I wake with a start from my recurring nightmare.

22 CRESS

On Sunday morning, Mom pops by early. She tells me to head out and take some me time. "I'm fine, Mom," I tell her, but she gives me *the* mom look. "Fine, I'll see if Ave is free for brunch."

"Good," Mom says, and she heads into the kitchen, no doubt making banana pancakes for Lexi.

Picking up my phone, I text Ave.

Cress: *Wanna do something crazy today?*

I've just stepped out of the shower when my phone rings and it's Ave. "Hey hey, lady."

"Hey, so what's this crazy adventure you have in mind?"

"Weeell, I wanna get a tattoo today and you are going to get one too." The line goes quiet, I pull it from my ear to see if we are still connected. "You still there, Ave?"

"Yeah," she answers.

"So, what do you say?"

"I can't believe I'm saying this but sure, I'm in."

I squeal in delight. "Great, I'll text you the address and meet you there."

"Sounds good, see you soon, Crazy Cress."

"Crazy Cress, I like that."

Two hours later, I'm sitting across from Ave, after our tattoos we, well I, decided that we'd get brunch too. I'm sipping on my coffee after eating my weight in waffles.

"I cannot believe I let you talk me into it," she says, popping a grape into her mouth.

"I cannot believe you agreed," I say, as I grab her wrist and look at her new ink under the wrapping, "but seriously, Ave, I have never seen you so happy. I think a certain sexy Irish doctor was just the medicine you needed."

"And I think a certain Channing Tatum looking doctor is the prescription you need." My eyes bug open, so she does know something. "One of these days, you are going to have to tell me what's up between you two."

I mime zipping my lips. "My lips are sealed." Then I lean forward. "But I will say—" I don't get to finish what I was going to say cause come crazy bitch slaps Ave across the face, yelling about some dude named Kye.

Before either of us have a chance to reply, she's storming away.

"What the fuck was that?" I question her. "And who the fuck is Kye?"

She shakes her head, cupping her cheek. "Beats me who Kye is. But, man, does she have a wicked left hook."

We finish our brunch but the atmosphere has changed since our encounter with Rocky Balboa and we decide to call it quits. We say our goodbyes and I head home to my munchkin and Mom. I'm looking forward to chillaxing on the sofa and preparing for the week ahead.

A couple days after my brunch date with Ave, I'm sitting at home when my phone rings, I don't recognize the number, without thinking, I swipe and answer, "Hey, this is Cress."

"Cressida, it's Flynn," he says, his Irish accent really thick and ohh so sexy.

"Hey, Doc, and I've told you to call me Cress.

"Okay. Hi, Cress, it's Flynn."

"Much better," I tease. "To what do I owe the pleasure of this call?"

"It's Avery—"

"What's wrong?" I say, sitting upright, my heart racing as I await his reply.

"We are at Western General. Bay is here."

"Ohh shit. I'll get Mom to watch Lexi. Be there soon."

Hanging up, I grab my bag, and tell Lexi she's heading to Nanna's and I need to go out for a bit. I call Mom after strapping Lexi into her car seat and tell her I'm on my way and what's happened. When I pull up at Mom's, she's waiting out front for me.

Climbing out, I unstrap Lexi, and she runs inside. Mom envelops me in a hug and tells me that everything will be fine and to keep her updated.

Racing to the hospital, I find a parking spot. Before

climbing out, I grab my phone and text Flynn to let him know I've arrived.

CRESS: *Just parked. Meet me in the ER.*
FLYNN: ***thumbs-up emoji***

Growling when I see the thumbs-up emoji—emojis are fun but a thumbs-up is just plain rude. I shake my head and race into the hospital to meet Flynn. A few moments after I arrive, I see him and shout as soon as I see him, "Flynn, how's our girl?"

"I don't know. She seems off. Doesn't seem herself," he says, his voice laced with concern.

"That's understandable, her sister is in the hospital and unconscious." I say, hoping to ease his worries.

"Yeah, I get that, but I don't know. I can't put my finger on it. I'm hoping you being here will put her at ease and pull her out of her funk."

"If I know Avery, she'll be putting on a brave front but on the inside, she'll be screaming and falling apart. She and Bay may not be in the best place right now but at the end of the day, Bay is her sister, and that means everything to Avery. Family always comes first is her motto."

He nods his head in agreement but he's clearly worried. "Let's go then."

As soon as we enter Bay's room, I race over to Ave and wrap my arms around her. She's stiff, even when Flynn embraces her. My eyes roam over her and I can feel what Flynn is sensing. Something is off with my best friend right now and it's more than her sister being attacked. Then I look at her arms and it hits me, it's Baylor standing before me and Avery is in that bed. *Fucking bitch* is pretending to be her, I need to get to the bottom of this and she's more likely to talk/confess if Flynn isn't here.

"Flynn, can you get Ave some water, she looks parched and dehydrated," I ask him, I need him out of this room so I can confirm my suspicions.

He nods and kisses Bay/Ave. "Be right back." My blood boils when he kisses her, *fucking bitch-faced cunt.*

The door closes behind Flynn and I stare at Baylor. "You're pretending to be her, aren't you, Baylor?"

"Am not," she scoffs in reply and that adds to my suspicion. That's how Baylor would talk, not Ave.

"Please, you lying bitch. The person lying in that bed is Avery Evans. Standing before me is bitchy Baylor Evans." *Once a bitch, always a bitch*, I think to myself as I stare at her. "You are not her," I growl at her, anger building that she's doing this. Why she's doing this?

"Am so!" Baylor yells back, her reply once again reconfirming my suspicion that Bay is playing games again.

Before I lose my shit with this bitch, the door opens and Flynn snarls, "Enough!" Clearly our yelling garnered some attention, and I'm still no closer to proving that Ave is in that bed.

His eyes flit between Baylor and me. "You are not Ave," I say again, poking Baylor in the chest.

"Yes, I am!" Baylor yells back, but I notice her voice waivers.

Pointing at Baylor, my anger builds, "You are not Avery Evans, I bet my life on it." She smacks my hand viciously away.

Flynn yells at us both, I've never heard him angry like this. I know this commotion isn't good for Ave, but I need to get everyone to see that this is Baylor and not Avery.

"Yeah, Cressida," Baylor sasses and it's with these two

words that I know I'm one-hundred-percent correct and from the look on Flynn's face, he too is starting to doubt the bitch before me.

Pointing at Baylor, I tell Flynn, "That is Baylor standing there." Then I stare down at my best friend in the bed. Lifting my gaze, I glare at Baylor before looking to Flynn. "Flynn, the person in that bed is Avery. My best friend. Your girlfriend. I know it without an ounce of doubt." I pause waiting for him to agree, but he still looks conflicted. "Flynn, I swear to you on my life. On Lexi's life, the person in that bed is Avery."

"Prove it," Baylor snarls.

"With pleasure," I say with glee. "Yesterday morning, Ave and I got tattoos." Grabbing the hem of my shirt, I show my new tattoo. As I look at my new ink, I smile. On my left hip, is a pink and blue inkblot with Lexi's name in the center in her handwriting. "I got this yesterday. Ave, the real Avery, got one on her wrist."

Baylor quickly hides her arms behind her back. *Busted, you stupid bitch*, I think to myself as her face drains of all color. Even when Flynn confronts her, she still tries to play off that she's Ave.

"I don't have to prove anything." She pleads, "I'm Avery. I'm your girlfriend. Flynn, please…"

"Uhh, yeah, you do," I say, stepping toward Baylor. The urge to hit her is strong and had Preston not wrapped his arms around me, I would have. I was so worked up that I didn't even notice he'd entered the room.

"Down, girl," he whispers into my ear, his voice instantly calms me and I melt back into him.

Closing my eyes, I take a deep breath and compose myself. Opening my eyes again, I watch as Flynn goes over to Ave and lifts the blanket covering her hand. As soon as he realizes that the person in the bed is Ave, he kisses her knuckles. Her eyes open and I think I stop breathing at seeing this. "It's okay, lass, I'm here," Flynn croons, as he continues to kiss her knuckles. Relief etched all over his face, he really does love her.

My eyes well with tears at the scene before me, that is until Bay steps toward Ave and says she's sorry. She thinks one word, five letters, will make this all okay. The more she says sorry, the more my anger builds again. "Are you shitting us right now, Bay?" I snap. "Sorry, really? That's all you've got? You better start talking now, bitch, and don't even think about lying to us."

"Shut it, Cressida," Baylor snaps at me. "No one asked for your opinion and no one wants you here now. Go home to your bastard child. You aren't needed."

I see red at her words and I lunge for her. Luckily for her, Preston holds me back because I'm ready to tear shreds off of her right now.

Once again, Flynn bellows at Baylor and me. I know he's right but I can't help it, my best friend was attacked. She's lying in a hospital bed and the bozos responsible are still out there, and to top it off, her bitch of a sister pretended to be her.

Flynn asks Preston to get the officers in here. He nods. "Sure, no worries." He looks to Ave. "Glad you're awake, Avery." He then turns to me. "Come on, Cress."

I roll my eyes at him, but from the look on his face, I know not to defy him right now. "Fine," I huff. Walking to the bed, I reach out and squeeze Ave's hand in mine. "I'll be right outside. I'm so mad at you right now, but I'm also glad you're okay." Kissing Ave on the cheek, I glare at Baylor and walk out of the room with Preston close behind me.

"Love, you need to calm down," he says as soon as the door closes.

"Do not tell me to calm down. My best friend was attacked and her whore of a sister pretended to be her. I think I'm allowed to be pissed off."

The door to Ave's room opens and Flynn steps out, in sync Preston and I turn around as Flynn walks over to us. "Everything all right?" Preston asks.

"Yeah. Ave wants to speak to Baylor."

"And you left her alone with that psycho bitch? I don't trust her," I say through gritted teeth. "One word and I'll take her skanky ho ass down."

"You've got a live one there, dude," Flynn says to Preston. He clearly knows about us and then I feel guilty that I haven't spoken to Ave about Pres and me. I guess now isn't the time but as soon as she's out of the hospital, it's time to tell her about us.

Preston shrugs and winks at me, I roll my eyes at him and shake my head. "Flynn, are you sure it's okay to leave them alone together?"

He nods his head. "Yeah, they'll be fine. I trust that Ave can handle her sister."

I nod and smile. "Yeah, if anyone can handle Bay, it's Avery. Look, I'm going to head to her place and grab a few things for her, I'll be back soon."

"Thanks, Cress."

Turning on my heel, I leave the two of them and head to my car. As I climb into my car, I realize I didn't say goodbye to Preston, and then I start to feel like a bitch.

CRESS: *Sorry for not saying bye.*

CRESS: *I just need to process all of this*

PRESTON: *It's okay, Love. Be sure to find me when you get back. Love you*
CRESS: *Love you too*

How does that man do it? With one text message he's calmed me down. Pulling out of my parking spot, I race to Ave and Baylor's to grab some things for her.

An hour later, I've dropped Ave her things. She looks better already and says that she'll be fine. Bitchy Baylor is nowhere to be seen, thank God for that. Like he has a sixth sense for me, Preston walks down the hallway when I exit Ave's room.

"Hey," I say, as I look up and see him.

"Hey, you calm now?"

"I was always calm."

"Liar liar pants on fire. I could feel the rage simmering when you were in my arms."

"If Flynn was in that bed and his twin did that, wouldn't you be all stabby and ragey too?"

"Yeah, I guess so," he says.

"No guessing about it." I pause and look up at him. "Can I have a hug?"

"Always," he says, wrapping his arms around my waist. He pulls me into him, I rest my head on his chest and slide my arms around him. His embrace relaxes me and since I got that call from Flynn, I finally relax. Lifting my head, I look up at him and smile. "What time do you get off?"

"I can get off anytime I want," he says with a wink, "But my shift finishes in about an hour."

"Can you stay at my place tonight?"

"Of course." He leans down and presses his lips to mine. I open my mouth and kiss him back. I know we are in the middle of the hospital but right now, I don't care. I need Preston like I need my next breath. "I love you," I whisper against his lips.

"I love you too."

Resting my head back on his chest, I close my eyes. I feel happy, content, and loved.

23 PRESTON

Wow, what a day.

Attacks, identity swapping, and a kid who thought he could fly like Superman off the front balcony of his house. FYI, he couldn't and ended up with a compound fracture to his left leg, a snapped wrist, and surgery.

My crazy day is finally over and I'm on my way over to see Cress and Lexi, which is now the best way to end a hectic day. But most of all, I want to see my girls. As I approach my car, I see someone leaning against it. Their head is down and I don't know who it is. "Can I help you?" I ask. They lift their head and when I see who it is, I sigh. "Get off my car," I growl, coming to a stop in front of him.

"Stay the fuck away from them." He snarls.

"Or what?"

"Don't test me, doctor boy. I can make your life a living fucking hell."

"I think I'll let Cress decide if she wants me in her life.

You better be careful or she will put you out of her life. She's already kicked you out of her bed." That was a low blow but this guy has pissed me off.

"I'll be back between her thighs soon enough, fucking her tight cunt. She's a fucking whore, one dick won't be enough for her. Just you wait."

"How can you speak about her like that? Cress is the most amazing mother and woman I know."

"Fuck off she is. She's a whore. Plain and simple. You are just the latest fucker to fall under the spell of her pussy."

"Warning noted. Now, get the fuck off my car. Don't make me tell you again."

He pushes himself off my car and stops in front of me. I can feel his breath on my face. He stares at me and I notice his eyes are dilated, bloodshot, and glassy. The trifecta when it comes to drug use, he is on something pretty strong. My guess would be coke.

"Stay the fuck away or I will make life really hard for the bitch." He shoves me in the chest and staggers away.

Turning around, I watch him skulk out of the parking garage. That man really gets on my nerves. Once he's out of sight, I climb into my car and head over to see my girls.

On the drive over I contemplate telling Cress about Creed's threats to me, but she has enough going on so I decide to keep it to myself for now. I will do everything I can to protect Cress and Lexi.

Knocking on the door, I wait for it to open. When it does, I smile when I see Lexi. She looks tired. "You okay, Princess Lexi? You look flushed."

"What does that mean?"

"A bit red in the cheeks."

"I just raced to open the door. Mommy said we

couldn't eat 'til you got here, so I was excited when I heard you." She grabs my hands. "Come on, we can eat now." She pulls me inside and shouts, "Moooooooomm, he's here…dinner."

A laugh escapes me as she drags me into the kitchen. Taking a seat at the table, I look at the spread before me and grin. Working long hours, I don't often get home-cooked meals, so I feel like a king and I can't wait to dive into the roast chicken, with all the veggies, and fresh dinner rolls.

"Hey, Love," I say to Cress as she walks into the kitchen.

"Hey," she says, placing a quick kiss on my lips before she sits next to me. She looks tired and drained.

"You okay?" I ask, reaching over to take her hand in mine. She looks down at our joined hands and then up at me again, something is going on because her eyes are dull right now.

"Yeah, just a lot going on."

"Do you want to talk about it?"

She looks to Lexi, then back at me. "Maybe later."

"It's a date." I smile at her and for the first time since I arrived, she smiles. That light is back in her eyes. I stare at her, she really is the most beautiful woman in the world.

"Can we eat now?" Lexi asks.

"Yes, Munchkin, we can." Cress dishes up and the three of us dig in.

After eating everything on my plate, I lean back in my chair. "Oh My God," I say, resting my hands on my stomach, "Cress, that was the best meal ever."

"You better have saved room for dessert."

Looking to her, I raise my eyebrows. *I'd love to have her for dessert.*

"It's not that," she laughs, "Lexi and I made apple crumble."

"Mommy let me sprinkle the cimmamon."

"Are you trying to fatten me up?"

Her eyes drift to my dick, she looks at me and shrugs. 'Minx,' I mouth. She blows me a kiss and stands up to grab dessert. My eyes watch her ass as she walks away. I lick my lips, she really does have the finest ass in the history of sexy asses.

After the best apple crumble I have ever eaten, I clean up the kitchen while Cress gets Lexi ready for bed. I've loaded the last dish in the dishwasher when she comes out. "Hey, can you have a look at Lexi's leg? The cut is taking forever to heal and she says it still hurts."

"Sure." I follow her into Lexi's bedroom. Sitting on the edge of her bed, I look at the cut. It's a little red around the edges and inflamed. "How long has it been like this?"

"I only noticed it tonight."

"Okay, let's wash it again and I'll pop some antiseptic onto it. Over the next few days, keep an eye on it. If it doesn't heal in a day or two, I'll prescribe some antibiotics for her."

"Should I be worried?" Cress questions.

Shaking my head. "Nah, it looks okay to me. I don't think we need to worry." That seems to ease her worry.

Cress and I tuck Lexi in and then I take her to bed. I make love to her before drifting off to sleep with the woman I love tucked into my side.

24 CRESS

THE FOLLOWING WEEK IS CRAZY AND I'M NOT JUST REFERRING to the taunts from Creed. The week started out with me picking up some sub work. Mom was only too happy to watch Lexi for me and on Wednesday, when she was stuck, Preston swooped in and saved the day. He picked Lexi up and the two of them spent the afternoon together. When I got home, I found them inside a blanket fort watching, *DuckTales*—I think Lexi now has a new favorite show. I don't think it's so much the show, it's that Preston likes it and she likes Preston very much.

Kicking off my shoes, I join them in the fort and snuggle in. Completely content and sated with Lexi and Preston. I'm currently in my happy place with the two people I love the most.

There's a knock at the door but no one wants to move so we ignore it, we stay in our fort watching *DuckTales*. The knocking stops and then my phone blows up with text message after text message. I shield them from Lexi but

Preston being Preston, he glances at the screen. His jaw clenches and he growls low in his throat as he reads the messages.

CREED: *Open your fucking door, bitch*
CREED: *Stop being a whore and answer me*
CREED: *Cressida fucking Bayliss, do not ignore me*
CREED: *Fuck you, bitch*
CREED: *I want to see Lexi tomorrow. Let me or else you will pay*
CRESS: *I'm working tomorrow, you can collect her from school*
CREED: *Maybe we can have some fun when I drop her home*
CRESS: *I told you, not going to happen*
CREED: *Just give in and fuck me already*
CRESS: *Good night, Creed*

After texting with Creed, I'm on edge. I excuse myself from the fort and go to the kitchen. Grabbing a bottle of white from the fridge, I pour myself a glass.

"You okay?" Preston asks, as he wraps his arms around me from behind, pulling me into his chest. His embrace instantly calms me.

Placing my glass on the countertop, I place my arms on top of his and snuggle back into him. "Yeah, I'm fine."

"Cress, I know that when a woman says fine, she is anything but fine."

Spinning around, I drape my arms over his shoulders. "Seriously, I'm fine. Creed just doesn't like being told no, if I let him spend time with Lexi, he'll back off."

"Are you sure?"

Nodding my head, I smile. "I'm sure." But even as I

say those two words, I have no idea. I don't think Creed would hurt Lexi but then again, I have never seen him like this before. I really don't know what to do.

Preston and I get Lexi off to bed and then we grab the bottle of wine and head out to the back deck since it's a lovely night. Preston and I drink our wine in silence. Each of us in our own heads. When the bottle is finished, I offer for him to stay, but he declines since he needs to be at the hospital early. He kisses me goodbye and I watch as he drives away.

With a sigh, I lock the screen and front door before I climb into bed. My last thought before I drift off to sleep is that I wish I'd met him first and he was Lexi's dad.

The next afternoon when I get home from school, I decide to clean the house so that tomorrow I can spend the entire day with Lexi. I turn on Spotify and get to it. Two hours later, I'm on the last job, vacuuming. "Shake it Off" by Taylor Swift comes on and I shake my booty around the living room as I finish the floor. I can feel eyes on me and when I look over to the door, I see Preston standing there, staring at me through the screen.

Jumping in fright, I rest my hand on my chest, "Dude, you scared the absolute shit out of me. Why didn't you knock?"

"And miss out on seeing you shake your booty, hell to the no."

Walking over to the door, I open the screen. As soon as I do, he slides his hand around my waist, pulls me to him, and presses his lips to mine. My leg lifts in that way they do in romantic movies. Our moment is interrupted when, Creed growls. "Are you finished tongue fucking my wife?"

Pushing away from Preston, I look to Creed. "I'm not your wife."

"Whatever." Creed looks to Preston. "Who the fuck are you?"

"Preston Knight," he says, offering his hand to Creed. "Pleasure to formally meet you, Creed."

My eyes widen at this, *Preston has met Creed before? When? And why did he not tell me?* Creed looks at Preston's hand and refuses to shake it. "So you're the asshole, she's slutting it up with."

"Excuse me," Preston fumes. "You don't speak to me, or Cress like that."

"Pres, I've got this," I say, resting my hand on his arm. He looks to me and nods. I can see the anguish in his face, he wants to protect me but he knows this is my fight. I smile up at him. Then I hear a little voice, "Mommy."

Looking down, I see Lexi walk up the stairs behind Creed. "Hey, Munchkin," I say, dropping down to my knees and opening my arms to her. She walks over and hugs me tight; she seems sad.

"Hi, Mommy."

"Did you have fun with Daddy Creed?" He growls at that name and I can't help but smirk at my slight win. She shrugs at me and my heart breaks for my little girl right now. She's never returned from being with Creed sad like this. "Why don't you go put your things away. I'll be there in a moment."

"Okay, Mommy," she sadly says. She looks to Creed. "Bye, Daddy Creed." Then she turns around and races inside.

"What happened? Why is she sad?"

"She wouldn't stop talking about the fucker standing next to you. I told her that he'll move on soon, no one hangs around a slut like you." I can feel the anger radiating from Preston, I step between him and Creed, the last thing I need is a fight breaking out between the two of them.

"Creed," I yell, "You cannot say shit like that to her. She's a little girl for fuck's sake."

"Well, it's the truth. If we arrived a few minutes later, you would have been fucking him right here in the doorway. I'm not sure this is a suitable environment for my daughter to be in anymore."

"Fuck you, Creed," I seethe through clenched teeth. "I'm the one who has been here for her ever since I found out I was pregnant. You pop in whenever you feel like it. You taunt me when you don't get your way and now, you are referring to me as a slut to my daughter. Some father figure you are."

"She's my daughter too," he snaps back.

"She might have your DNA but you certainly are no father."

"What? And he is?" He flicks his finger toward Preston.

"He's more of a father than you ever will be."

"Don't push me, bitch." I feel Preston step forward at this, I block him but I don't know how much longer I can hold him back. "If I want to, I can make your life a living hell, Cressida. Just you remember that." His gaze roams over my body and I shudder at the lewdness in his gaze. "See you round, Dollface."

He blows me a kiss and walks away. Leaving me

fuming. "Cress," Preston says from next to me, "are you okay?"

Nodding my head, I bite my thumbnail. "I need you to leave."

"What?" he shouts. "Why?" Preston reaches for me and I pull back.

"I need you to go, Preston. I need to focus on Lexi right now."

"Cress—"

"No," I shout. "Preston, I need time to think. Please?" I plead, cupping his cheek in my palm, I stare at him. "Please, I need to focus on Lexi tonight."

"I don't like this but if you insist."

"I do, I need some alone time with Lexi tonight. My little girl needs me."

"I'll give you tonight, Cress, but I'm not going anywhere. You, me, and Lexi, we belong together like Huey, Dewy, and Louie belong with Scrooge."

He kisses me on the temple and walks out. Standing in the doorway, I watch him climb into his car and drive away. Closing the door, I lock it and engage the deadlock. Turning around, I slide down the wood and rest my head on my knees. Did I just push the best thing to ever happen to us away?

My phone pings with a text, without looking, I know it's Creed. Pulling it out of my pocket, I open and read his messages, instantly regretting opening it.

CREED: *I'm better than that doctor asshole, he will not take my place in Lexi's life. You try and push me out and I will file for custody.*
CREED: *I know people and those people will ruin you.*
CREED: *Don't push me*

Tears well in my eyes as I read his texts over and over. "Mommy," Lexi says from the hall. Looking up, I see her standing there staring at me.

"What's up Munchkin?" I say, as I stand up and wipe at my eyes.

"Where's Prince Dr. Preston?"

"He had to go home."

"Ohh," she sadly says.

"How was your afternoon with Daddy Creed?"

"I didn't have fun. He was kinda mean when I talked about Prince Dr. Preston and *DuckTales*."

"Don't let that worry you. How about we build another fort, watch *DuckTales* and eat mac 'n' cheese in the fort?"

"Can we sleep in there too?"

"It's a school night tonight, but maybe we can on the weekend?"

"Really?" Her eyes widen in delight.

"Of course, Munchkin."

"Yesss," she squeals, her little face lit up with joy.

"You get the pillows. I'll get the blankets." Before I've finished saying that, she's racing away and just like that, my daughter is happy.

For the next few hours, I focus on Lexi and I forget all about Creed's threats, but guilt from pushing Preston away begins to fester.

After watching a whole season of *DuckTales* and eating our weight in mac 'n' cheese, I bathe Lexi and get her off to bed…leaving me alone with my thoughts and guilt.

Pouring myself a glass of wine, I curl up on the sofa. I grab my iPad to read but my mind keeps drifting to Preston, and specifically how I spoke to him. How I pushed him away. And how he said he's not going anywhere. I feel like a total bitch and now, I need to apologize. Looking at the clock, I realize he'll be sleeping but I text him anyway, this way he can wake up to an apology message.

> **CRESS:** *I'm so sorry, Preston. I acted like a total whorebag bitch. I took my fears and anger out on you, and I shouldn't have done that.*
> *I'm so sorry.*
> *Please know that I love you with all my heart and soul. I've never felt like this about anyone before. It's been Lexi and me for so long and I freaked out at the prospect of losing her. Until I met you, she was my everything. Now you both hold that spot in my heart.*
> **CRESS:** *I'll see you soon…Gotta go, buffalo Xo*
> **CRESS:** *PS. I'll leave the corny sign-offs to you…that was really bad*
> **CRESS:** *PPS. Love you long-time*

I hit send and I really do hope I see him again soon. I really hope Creed hasn't ruined this for me.

25 PRESTON

Preston, I need time to think. Please?

Preston, I need time to think. Please?

Preston, I need time to think. Please?

Those seven words play on a loop in my head. The look of hurt on her face at Creed's words gutted me. Her sending me away gutted me. I've fallen hard for this woman and even though she just pushed me away, I know I've finally found 'the one.' It's fucking crazy to be talking like this after such a short period of time, and considering she sent me away tonight, but when you know, you know.

Cress is it for me.

Lexi too. I love that little girl as if she were my own.

My phone pings with a text, picking it up, I see it's from Cress. As I read her words, a smile graces my face and I know we'll be fine.

PRESTON: *No need to apologize. It was a rough*

afternoon. I love you too. I'll pop round after my shift tomorrow.

She texts me back immediately.

CRESS: *I promise to make it up to you*
PRESTON: *Naked horizontal tango? **wink wink***
CRESS: *That can be arranged. I'd do anything for you, Preston, anything!*
CRESS: *I love you unconditionally.*
CRESS: *Nite nite, Preston*
PRESTON: *I'd do anything for you and Lexi too. I hope you know that.*
PRESTON: *Love you xo*
PRESTON: *Nite, Queen Cress*

Placing my phone on the side table, I lie back and finally relax. *I love you unconditionally* are the four new words now playing over in my mind as I drift off to sleep.

The next day, I'm called into Dr. Jenkins' office. She's sitting behind her desk, her shoulder-length dark hair straight as usual when I enter. She pushes up her glasses and smiles as I enter. "Preston, how are you?" she asks, as she walks around her desk and ushers me to the seating area in her office. Perks of being chief, a nice large office.

"Good, today was quiet so it was a good paperwork day."

"You better not have jinxed it by saying the 'Q' word." We both laugh. "You are probably wondering why I called you in here today." I nod my head. "I've heard that Boston," my eyes widen that she knows, "is interested in you leading their new pediatric wing. I want to know what I can do to entice you to stay."

"How did you know? They only emailed the offer a few days ago, and I haven't spoken to anyone about it yet."

"It's my job to know, Preston. I didn't get to this position because I slept my way here. I got it because I'm the best, as are you. I don't want to lose you. The hospital doesn't want to lose you. So, what will it take for you to stay?"

"I...I—" I'm stumped, I have no idea what to say right now.

"Think it over and get back to me."

Standing up, I shake her hand and walk out, thankful that my shift is over because I have a lot to think about but before I can think about work, I need, no want, to go see my girls.

Jumping into my car, I drive over to Cress's. I pull up and there's a gray sedan parked out front. Looking to the house, I see Cress talking with a guy in a suit. Climbing out of my car, I walk up to them. Cress looks pale. "Cress, Love," I ask, "is everything okay?"

She looks at me blankly and nods. Then she looks back to the man, "As I said, Agent Cox, apart from handover with my daughter, I don't know what Creed gets up to. Hell, I don't even know where he lives."

"Okay, thank you for your time." He hands her a card. "If you think of anything else, please don't hesitate to contact me."

"What have you gotten yourself into Creed?" she whispers to herself after I close the door. Escorting her to the sofa, I sit next to her.

"What was that all about?"

"He's an agent with the DEA. Seems Creed is into some bad shit, he was questioning me about him."

"Fuck, seriously?"

"Yep, just when I think it can't get worse regarding him, this happens."

"What are you going to do?"

"What can I do?"

"Maybe you need to speak to a lawyer?"

"I can't afford that."

"I'll help you if you need," I offer.

She shakes her head and takes my hand in hers. "Thanks, but I can't take your money. I'll figure this out."

Her response doesn't surprise me at all. "Well, my offer is there any time."

"Thank you," she says. She looks at me, my cock twitching at the heat in her eyes. "Now, where's my hello kiss?"

"I'm so sorry." Reaching over, I pull her onto my lap and press my lips to hers. Breaking the kiss I rest my forehead on hers. "Hi."

"Hi," she replies with a smile. "How was your day?"

"Crazy."

"DEA crazy?"

"Not that crazy but still crazy. I got a job offer—"

"That's amazing, Preston. Congrats."

"It's umm ahh, in Boston."

"Ohh," she says, no longer elated at my news. "So you're moving?"

"I don't know. My boss here offered me anything I want to stay here in Chicago."

"Wow, that's great. What are you going to do?"

I shrug. "I don't know. Leading a pediatric unit would be amazing, but my life is here...you and Lexi are here."

She shakes her head. "No, don't base your decision on us." I go to interrupt but she places her finger on my lips.

"You need to do what's best for you and your career. I would never stop you from doing that, BUT in saying that, I really hope you stay cause I kinda like having you around." She grinds herself on me, my cock hardening beneath her.

"God, I love you," I say, leaning over I press my lips to hers. Before she can process what's happening, I flip her onto her back, cocooning her under me on the sofa. "What time is your mom dropping Lexi home?"

"Any minute now."

"Dammit, I'll just have to settle for this for now." Pressing my lips to hers, I fuck her mouth with my tongue. She moans into my mouth, and my cock hardens further between us, painfully pressing against my zipper. She swivels her hips, pressing against my dick harder. "Cress," I warn into the kiss. She giggles against my lips and continues to circle her hips. "You are a minx," I say, nipping her bottom lip between my teeth. I slide my hand between us and up under her skirt. I cup her pussy, pressing my thumb into her clit. This is pretty steamy but I can't stop what I'm doing. I need to be inside of her now.

"Yes," she mewls, closing her eyes. Her head drops back elongating her neck, leaning down I lick from her shoulder to under her ear. "Fuck me, Preston," she whispers, pulling her panties to the side, I'm about to push my finger inside when the front door swings open and Lexi yells, "Mooooommmy, I'm home."

Cress freaks out and shoves me off her. I land on my back on the floor with a thud. "Uggh," I groan. Looking up at her, her cheeks are flushed and she's never looked more beautiful.

"Duck, I'm so sorry," she says, her comment sets me off and I start to laugh. She laughs too.

"Mommy. Prince Dr. Knight. What's so funny?" Lexi asks, this causes us both to laugh even harder.

"Come on, sweetheart," Momma Cress says. "Let's unpack your bag and then Mommy and Doc P. will get you that snack I promised."

"Okay, Nanna."

Lexi skips off. Momma Cress looks down at us, shakes her head, and smirks. She follows after Lexi while Cress and I continue to laugh. I feel like a teenager getting busted again.

Once composed, Cress and I hop up. Pulling her into my arms, I hug her. "I love you," I whisper into her hair.

"I love you too." She kisses my cheek and heads into the kitchen to prepare Lexi her snack.

Taking a seat at the island, I watch Cress flit about the kitchen. She looks happy, and I realize I don't want to ever see her unhappy again. I don't think I'm going to accept Boston. But before I make up my mind, I need to talk to Dr. Jenkins and see if she was serious. I think I have an idea that will benefit both myself and the hospital.

"Cress," I say. "I need to go. I'll call you later."

Placing a kiss on her cheek, I squeeze her ass and walk out, passing Lexi and Momma Cress on the way. "I'll see you ladies later."

Racing down the path to my car, I look up and see Creed leaning against the hood. "Creed." I growl, anger building as he pushes off and steps toward me.

"Clearly my words the other week fell on deaf ears and that bitch, or you, haven't heeded any of my messages. Stay the fuck away."

"And if I remember correctly, I told *you* to stay away. Cress and Lexi are better off without you in their life."

"I'm her father, you can't stop me from seeing Lexi and

if you try, I will make life difficult for the bitch, and you. Last chance, fucker."

"You don't scare me, Creed."

"You should be scared, Doc. I know people and with one call, I can make you disappear, or even better, I can ruin your career. Don't test me."

"Warning noted. Now, get the fuck off my car."

Not wanting to engage with him any further, I walk around to the driver's side and unlock my car. I stare at him over the roof of my car. "Maybe it's you who needs to stay the fuck away. Leave Cress and Lexi alone to live their lives."

"Fuck you, asshole." He flips me the bird and saunters down the street like his shit don't stink.

Climbing into my car, I sit and watch him slither into his piece of shit car and drive away. With a sigh, I start my car and head to the hospital. Once I've spoken with Dr. Jenkins, I'll deal with Creed and his threats. I will not let him or anyone hurt those I love.

26   CRESS

PRESTON HAS STAYED AT MY PLACE EVERY NIGHT THIS WEEK and each night after making love, I've fallen asleep wrapped in his arms. Thankfully, I haven't had that horrible nightmare. He has slipped into our life perfectly. It's like he's always been a part of our family. Watching him with Lexi fills my heart with so much joy.

Each morning, we make breakfast together and then go our separate ways. I'm in the middle of the grocery store on Tuesday when I get a phone call from Lexi's school, telling me she's unwell and I need to come and get her.

Abandoning my shopping cart, I race to the school to pick her up. As soon as I see her, I know something is terribly wrong. She's clammy and pale. Her breathing is labored and her heart is racing. I take her straight to Western General and call Preston on the way.

As soon as we arrive, like when she cut herself, he's waiting for us. He opens the back door and I swear I hear him mumble, "Shit." Lexi is whisked inside, I leave my car out front, I don't care if it gets towed; my daughter needs me.

It's chaotic, Preston and Andi immediately spring into action. The two of them work in sync like a well-oiled machine. I watch from the sidelines, helpless to do anything. Lexi is admitted to the children's ward immediately and when this happens, I know it's bad. They insert an IV, run tests and other things, but I'm too emotional to focus right now.

Things have settled down and now we wait for the results to come in. I sit by her bed and stare at her little body in the bed, biting my thumbnail. It's amazing how quickly she got sicker, I feel like a crap mom for not focusing on her more. I should have known something was up when I dropped her at school this morning. I should have known. Lexi is sound asleep right now. Her chest rising and falling as she breathes. Her skin is so pale and she looks sick, really really sick.

How did I miss this?

A few hours later, Preston enters Lexi's room. From the look on his face, I know it's not good. My world crumbles around me when Preston says, "Cress, Lexi has sepsis."

Collapsing to the floor, the tears break free. "Nooooo," I cry.

Preston takes me into his arms and I cry. "Cress," he quietly says, "we need to move Lexi up to ICU. Then we will need to do a spinal tap so we know exactly what infection we are working with. While we wait for the sepsis workup, we will administer a broad spectrum antibiotic and as soon as we get the results, we will change her antibiotic to treat the specific infection." I listen to him speak but nothing he says really registers, he's in full-on doctor mode right now. He's serious and to see him like this, adds to my fears for Lexi.

"Will she be okay?" I ask.

He looks at me. "I will do everything I can to make sure she is."

"Will. She. Be. Okay?" I ask again. "Preston, tell me the truth," I snap.

"I can't tell you what you want to hear right now, Cress, but know that I'm doing everything I can."

"Well, do more!" I shout. "I can't lose her, Preston. I just can't."

"Cress," he pleads.

"Preston. You need to fix her. Please." Walking away from him, I sit next to her bed until Andi returns with an orderly so they can move her up to ICU.

Once she's settled in ICU, I take a breather. I step outside and lean against the wall, sliding down I sigh. I need my mom. Grabbing my phone, I call her. "Hi, Cress," Mom says when she answers.

"Mom," I blubber.

"What's wrong?"

"It's Lex, she in ICU."

"What's happened?"

Tears pour down my cheeks. "She has sepsis, Mom. How did I not know she was so sick? I'm the worst mom ever."

"Stop that nonsense," Mom says. "I'll swing by your place and pack you both some things. I'll be there soon. And, Cress?"

"Yeah?"

"She's strong. She's a Bayliss. Give her a kiss from Nanna and tell her I'll be there soon."

"Thanks, Mom."

Hanging up, I head back into ICU and I sit next to my little girl. Taking her little hand in mine, I bring it to my lips and kiss her knuckles. Her eyes flutter but she's so exhausted she can't open them. Running my hand across her forehead, I lean down and press my lips to her temple. "I love you, Munchkin. Please get better. Please."

Closing my eyes, I rest my head on the bed next to her and holding her hand in mine, I drift off to sleep. I'm woken when someone squeezes my shoulder. Turning my head, I see Creed standing there, the look on his face is murderous.

"Thanks for fucking letting me know she was in the hospital," he snarls.

"Creed."

"What lame-ass excuse do you have, huh? I had to find out from your mom that she was here. What the fuck, Cress?"

"Excuse me, sir," Andi says, "You need to calm down and curb the language."

"Ohh fuck off," he sneers. "This bitch here didn't tell me that my daughter was in the hospital."

"This woman," Andi says, "hasn't had a chance to."

"She called her fucking mother, she had time to call me. She's just being a bitch."

"Last warning, sir, you use language like that again and I will have no choice but to call security. Now, I suggest you leave and calm down. Once you are calm, you can come back. Lexi doesn't need this right now."

"Everything okay here?" Preston asks, as he walks in.

Creed looks to Preston and his face turns red. "I want a new fucking doctor," he snarls.

"Dr. Knight is the best that we have, sir," Andi says. "I assure you, your daughter is in excellent hands."

"As is my wife when it comes to this fucker."

"Creed," I snap. "Now is not the ducking time. Lexi needs us. If you want to stay, stop being a jackass and focus on her."

"Fuck this shit," he bellows and storms out of ICU, passing Mom in the doorway.

"Cress," Mom says, and as soon as I hear her voice, the tears start again.

"Mom," I cry, standing up I race over to her. Mom wraps her arms around me in the way only a mom can. Wrapping mine around hers, I cry into her shoulder.

"Shhhh," she coos. "It's all going to be okay."

"It's not, Mom, my baby is sick, so so sick and I missed it. I'm a shit mom."

"No, you are not. I won't let you talk like that. Now, you are going to go to the bathroom and wash your face. Then you will go to the cafeteria, get a coffee, and once you are calm, you will come back and be strong for your daughter."

"I'm not leaving her."

"Yes, you are," Mom says. "I will call security myself if I have to. You need to look after you too. Now go. Coffee. Now."

"Come on," Preston says. "I could do with a coffee too." He looks to Andi. "Please page me as soon as the results are in, or if anything changes."

"Can do, Bossman." She turns to walk way and then looks over her shoulder. "And take her across the road for coffee, the stuff in the cafeteria is shit."

He nods and takes my hand, normally that calms me but not this time. I'm so highly strung. All I want right now is for Lexi to get better. Reluctantly, I let him escort me over to the coffee shop because I know my mom, she really will call security if I don't go. Deep down, I know she's right. I need to calm down so I can focus and be here for Lexi.

27 PRESTON

CRESS AND I ARE SITTING IN THE COFFEE SHOP ACROSS THE road from the hospital, waiting for our drinks. She's biting her thumbnail, something I've noticed she does when she's anxious, sad, or her anxiety is through the roof. They call my name and I go get our drinks. I place Cress's coffee in front of her, she looks at it but doesn't pick it up. She goes back to staring into space. Her refusing coffee proves that she's not okay.

"Cress, Love, talk to me?" She looks at me, her mouth opens and closes a few times. "Please," I beg.

"You really want to know what I'm thinking right now?" I nod my head. "My daughter is in the in ICU," she sneers, "'cause I missed the signs. I'm her mom for fuck's sake. I should have known something was up. It's my fault. I should—"

"Cress, it's no one's fault."

"I'm not finished," she snaps. "I should have paid more attention. I should have been focusing on her one-hundred-percent of the time, not spending it with you." She pauses, takes a deep breath, and from the look in her eye, she's moved from anger to rage. "And then there's you. You're a fucking doctor, and you didn't see this happening right under your nose. How? How did you not see what was happening to my baby girl?" She pauses and swallows. "Preston," she cries. "How did this happen? How did we both miss this?"

Tears are pouring down her face. Hopping up from my chair, I walk over to her lift her up, sit back down, and wrap my arms around her. "Shhhh," I whisper. "Cress, you need to keep thinking positive. Lexi is tough. I will do everything I can to get her better."

"You promise?"

"Yes, I promise to do everything I can."

"No, promise me she will be okay?"

Shaking my head, I tell her honestly, "I can't promise she will be okay but, Cress, I won't rest until she's better."

"That's not enough. She needs more. I need more." She hops off my lap, walks out of the coffee shop, crosses the road, and heads back to the hospital.

Rubbing my forehead, I sigh. I want so much to tell her it will all be okay, but I can't. I never make a promise like that because I cannot guarantee it will be okay, but I promise I will do everything humanly possible to get Lexi well again. I wish I could promise what she wants, but I can't promise that, I just can't.

A voice from behind snarls, "Ohh look, she's finally seeing that you really are a fucking piece of shit."

"Creed," I say through clenched teeth. "Fuck off, I'm not in the mood for your shit."

"And I'm not in the mood to sit around a hospital

waiting for my daughter to get better 'cause you fucked up."

Standing up, I get in his face. "I didn't fuck up. This is no one's fault. Kids get sick, it's a part of life."

"You were too busy fucking that slut to see what was happening. You didn't see her getting sick right before your eyes 'cause that woman's cunt was all you could think about." The coffee shop falls silent, everyone's eyes are on Creed and me. He steps closer, his nose millimeters from mine. "You missed this, Knight, this is on you." He pokes my chest. "If my little girl dies, I will sue your ass for everything you have, *and* I'll make sure that Cress hates you with a vengeance."

Shoving him, he stumbles backward. I step toward him, my heart racing as my anger rises. I want to knock this fucker out. My blood is boiling at the words coming from his mouth. "Fuck off, you piece of shit. You don't care about Lexi or Cress." My fist clenches and I'm so close to hitting him. "Do everyone a favor and fuck off."

His eyes drop to my fist, his lip lifts in an evil smirk. "Go on, hit me. Just another thing to add to the list of things that you are going to go down for."

Raising my arm, I pull back ready to knock him out but someone covers my hand and stops me. "I don't know who you are," Flynn says, "but you need to walk away."

"Fuck you both," Creed snaps. "Enjoy your last days as a doctor, Knight." He storms out of the coffee shop. My eyes follow him as he walks down the street and away from the hospital.

Flynn stands in front of me and squeezes my shoulder. "You good?"

Looking at him, I shake my head side to side. "Not really, no."

"Wanna talk about it?"

"Not really, but I know you, you'll make me talk."

"Good, now start talking."

"I did fuck up, Flynn. I missed this. I'm a doctor for fuck's sake, how did I miss her being this sick?"

"I don't know the specifics but I do know you, you are a fucking great doctor, Preston."

"Tell that to that little girl in that hospital. To Cress, the woman I love. Lexi is in the ICU 'cause I didn't pick up on the signs. I should have looked at her cuts more. I should have done more. I should have—"

"Should have what?" Flynn snaps. He stares at me and I shrug because I really don't know what I could have done. "Exactly. Now, pull your head out of your ass and focus. There's no point in going over what-ifs right now. Right now, you need to concentrate on what you can see and do. Be the best doctor for Lexi and be there for Cress."

"She hates me right now."

"She doesn't hate you. She's just a mom who's worried about her daughter."

I stare at my best friend and process his words, I don't agree with him at all. "You're right," I say to placate him. "Lexi and Cress need me right now. They need me to be on top of my game so I can get her through this."

"That's the Preston I know."

We exit the coffee shop and head back to the hospital. I check in on Lexi, but there's been no change and until we get the work up, we won't know how to treat whatever she has effectively.

It's been two days since Lexi was admitted and I think I've slept for maybe four hours. I've set up camp in the doctors' lounge. Lexi is my only case right now, until she is out of the woods she is going to have all my attention. To make matters worse, my princess now has pneumonia too. Her little body is wilting away and it's all my fault. I should have picked up that Lexi wasn't well. This is on me and no matter what anyone says, this is my fault, but I will do everything in my power to make sure she makes a full recovery.

28　CRESS

I'VE LOST COUNT AS TO HOW MANY DAYS IT'S BEEN NOW; I think it's three, no four days, and there's been no improvement. Not only does my baby girl have sepsis from the cut on her arm, not her leg like I thought since that was the one she was complaining about. She now has pneumonia due to her already compromised respiratory system; damn the asthma that runs in the family.

I've just had a shower, at the insistance of Andi, Mom, and Ave. Avery and I have been texting constantly, I told her not to come. I can't handle seeing the anguish in her face too, and thankfully, she's doing as I asked. Earning her the title of 'bestest friend in the world.'

Walking back into Lexi's room, I lean against the doorframe and stare at her little body hooked up to all the machines. Emotion overcomes me at the sight of her. Racing to the side of the bed, I take a seat and stare down at her. Her cheeks have color today but she still sleeps a lot. "I'm so sorry, Munchkin," I whisper, brushing a tendril of hair off her face. "I've let you down. I will never let you down again, just please, please pull through. Please get better, please, Munchkin, please." Lowering my head to her bed, I cry. Gut-wrenching sobs break free as I let it all out.

This is all my fault.
This is all my fault.
This is all my fault.
This is all my fault.

I keep repeating this over and over as the tears continue to fall. A hand touches my back and I know whose hand it is. Lifting my head, I turn my head to see Preston staring down at me. He's got that 'I'm sorry' look and I'm sick of seeing that look on everyone's face.

"Cress—"

"No," I snap, standing up, I turn and face him, "If I hadn't have been fucking around with you," I poke him in the chest, "Lex would not be in that bed right now. This is all my fault." I pause. "Actually, it's all your fault."

"Cress, no, it's no one's fault." He tries to soothe me but deep down I know this is all my fault. I'm projecting my fear right now, but it feels good to be angry. If I focus on how mad I am, I don't dwell on the fact that I fucked up.

"I'm her mother, goddammit. I should I have seen her getting sick. I should have known." Dropping to my knees, I shake my head and cry. Looking up at Preston, I see anguish on his face, "I can't lose her, Preston. I can't. She's my everything." Another wave of sobs break free. "Please save my baby girl. Please, Preston, please."

He squats in front of me and envelops me in his arms. "Cress, I will do everything humanly possible to save her." His warmth and words are comforting and I lean into him.

Closing my eyes, I cry into his chest. My sobs have eased but I still feel like the shittiest mother in the world. Taking a deep breath, I pull back and look up at Preston, like always with us, that déjà vu feeling encompasses me and something passes between us. I can feel him giving me the strength I need to go on.

Movement by the door catches my attention and I look up into the glaring eyes of Creed.

"Creed, you're back," I say. Pushing away from Preston, I stand up and walk over to him. Preston follows, standing close behind me.

"I'm checking on *my* daughter," he snarls. "She still not any better?" He pauses but continues, not giving me a chance to talk. "I really think we need a new doctor, Baby-doll, the current one is clearly shit."

Preston tenses behind me. A lump forms in my throat at the harshness of his words but what surprises me most is, I wonder if he's right? Is Preston too close? Is our relationship compromising his care of Lexi?

"Do you want to sit with her for a bit?"

"Like you can fucking stop me," he snarls, stepping into the room. He walks past us and shoves his shoulder into Preston. Looking to Preston, I apologize with my eyes. It's no secret that Preston and Creed can't stand one another, actually no one can stand Creed. Not even Andi and she loves everyone.

"I'll stop in later," Preston says. "Text me if you need anything or there's any change. If it's urgent, get them to page me." He presses his lips to my temple. Closing my eyes, I draw strength from him. He exits the room and when I turn around, Creed is staring at me, I don't like the look in his eyes right now. Taking a deep breath, I walk over to the bed and sit. Creed sits and takes the chair on the opposite side.

"How is she?" he asks. I'm shocked at his question, he hasn't once asked about her. He normally just sits here and yells at everyone.

"There's been no change. The pneumonia was unexpected but her lungs will slowly get better. She's currently on several antibiotics but until they start working, it's a waiting game."

"How did this all happen?" he questions, not a hint of malice in his voice. It almost seems like he cares.

"I don't know," I dejectedly say.

"How can you not know, you're her fucking mother?" And there's the Creed I know.

"That's rich coming from her absentee father," I angrily snap back.

He stands up and holds on to the end of the bed. He stares at me and I shudder from his leering gaze. "Maybe it's time I see my lawyer about getting custody, since you seem to be doing such a stellar job."

Jumping to my feet, I race toward him. "Over my dead body will you ever get custody of Lexi."

"That can be arranged," he nonchalantly says, staring at me with a sinister smirk on his face. "Maybe it's time I become less absentee."

"Why, Creed, why? Why now, after five years, do you suddenly give a shit about her?"

"'Cause it fucks with your mind, Dollface, and fucking with you is a favorite hobby of mine and since I can no longer fuck you, I will fuck with you. I hold the power here, you should remember that." He steps toward me and grips my chin roughly. He glares at me. "Enjoy the time you have with her because when I'm done, you will have nothing. N-O-T-H-I-N-G. You will be begging for me and my cock, and guess what? I won't give you shit. You will be all alone and it's all yours and lover boy's fault because you couldn't look after my daughter." Before I can say anything, he presses his lips to mine. He grips my upper arms tightly, trying to gain access to my mouth. "Bitch," he snarls against my pursed lips before he turns on his heel, storming out of Lexi's hospital room.

"Ohh God," I cry, covering my mouth as his words sink in.

"Cress," Preston says from the doorway, "is everything okay?"

Spinning around I stare at Preston. Swallowing deeply, I storm over to him and lose it. "You are the reason Dickwad Dawson is threatening me. You should be fixing her quicker. You need to fix her now," I cry, hitting his chest with my palms. "You need to fix her," I cry.

"Cress—"

"NOW!" I interrupt and yell at him, "You need to fix her now because he's threatening to take my little girl from me. That's all on you." Pausing, I look at him, breathing heavily, "I want a new doctor on her case. I never want to see you again, Preston Knight. Get the fuck out of my daughter's hospital room. It's over. We are over."

"Cress, pl—"

"I said get the fuck out. Falling for you has caused all of this. This is all your fault, I hate you."

Turning away from him, I walk back to Lexi's bed and climb in next to her. I pull her close to me and cry.

I cry for Lexi.

I cry for losing Preston.

I cry because I hate Creed more than I ever thought possible.

And I cry for the shitshow my life has become.

Tears pour down my cheeks as I run my fingers through Lexi's hair. I've never been so scared in my entire life. I'm going to lose my daughter, and it's either going to be to the bacteria that's currently ravaging her little body, or to her dickwad of a father, and this is all Preston's fault. Quietly I murmur to myself, "Falling for Dr. Knight was the worst thing I have ever done."

29 PRESTON

"I want a new doctor on her case. I never want to see you again, Preston Knight. Get the fuck out of my daughter's hospital room."

Those words play on a loop over and over in my mind. And each time, it's more crushing than the last. Sliding down the wall next to Lexi's room, I run my fingers through my hair. Pulling the strands in frustration, the follicles tear, but it gives little reprieve to my mood.

"What are you doing on the floor?" Andi asks as she slides down to sit next to me.

"Cress kicked me out and I think we broke up. No, we did break up, she said it's over."

"She didn't mean it. That woman loves you unconditionally." She squeezes my arm in the reassuring way she always does, but this time there's no reassurance at all. "It's a trying time for all, Preston. Give her space and just be you, she'll be back in your arms in no time."

"When did you get so wise?"

"I've always been this wise. You are just noticing it now."

I smile at her. "Thanks, Andi."

"Anytime, but can I make a suggestion?"

"Sure."

"Go home and shower, you stink like a sewer rat."

"There's the Andi I know but I'm not leaving, my girls need me." And I mean that, I think of Lexi as my own.

"Preston," she snaps. "Go home and shower. You have been here for four days straight, you need a break and a shower. Then come back refreshed and ready to fight, both the sepsis and for your girls. You've just administered the antibiotics that are gonna kick this thing's ass, now IS the time to freshen up besides, Lexi doesn't need a stinky broody doctor around while she's recovering."

"I'm not broody."

"But you are admitting you stink? I promise to page if there's ANY change."

"Promise?"

"Yes, now go before I vomit. You reek and no one needs that."

A laugh escapes me and I stand up, looking into Lexi's room, I see Cress lying in bed with her. Her cheeks are wet from crying, turning around I come face-to-face with Creed. "Told you to stay away but looks like the bitch woke up and dumped your sorry ass."

"Fuck off, Creed."

"Don't worry, Doc, I'll take good care of her. I'll show her how a real man fucks."

I shake my head. "How you can be thinking about that right now when your daughter is in there fighting for her life is beyond me, but it also shows you know nothing about Cress. Dick, and especially yours, is the last thing on her mind right now. Now, if you excuse me, I need to get back to work."

Stepping around him, I walk away, ignoring the taunts he's yelling at my back. Passing Steve from security, I nod at him and give him the 'I'll leave him to you' look. Stopping, I turn and watch as Steve escorts a yelling and cursing Creed from the ICU.

Once he's removed from the ward, I head down to my car and race home. As soon as I walk inside, I stop when I see one of Lexi's *My Little Pony* figurines sitting on the entry table. I pick up the purple pony and whisper, "I'm sorry for letting you down, Lexi, I'm going to make you better…I hope."

Stepping into the shower, I close my eyes and let the hot water wash over me. Lifting my head, I smile when I see all of Cress's products in the nook. Flicking open the cap of her shower gel, I breathe it in. The lime and coconut smell reminds me so much of Cress and happier times. Turning around, I slide down the tiles and sit on the floor. Leaning my arms on the seat, I stare at the bottle in my hands. The ringing of my phone grabs my attention. I turn off the water, wrap a towel around my waist. Stepping in my bedroom, I pick my phone up off the bed. I see that it's my brother, Keeton, calling. I'm not in the mood to talk so I let it go to voicemail. Throwing it back on the bed, I walk back into the bathroom and dry off. Walking naked into the closet, I change back into black slacks and a white button-down.

My phone beeps with a text, I know it will be Keeton, he's a persistent son of a bitch, so I sit on the end of the bed and reply to him without reading his message.

PRESTON: *Super busy. Catch up soon*

KEETON: *Looking forward to it…it's been forever. Call when you can*
PRESTON: *Will do.*

Throwing a few changes of clothes into a bag, I grab a few toiletries and head back to the hospital. Dropping off my things in my locker, I head straight to ICU.

Walking into Lexi's room, I find it empty and my heart stops beating in my chest. I spin around and before I can ask, Andi says, "They've taken her for another chest X-ray and I managed to convince Cress to take a walk. She's just as stubborn as you, no wonder you two are in love."

"She broke up with me, remember?"

"She's not thinking clearly. One problem at a time, and no offense to your ego, but that little girl should be our number one focus right now."

"Stop being rational."

"I can't help it that I'm the only one thinking clearly right now." She turns and walks away. She stops, turns and says, "Ohh, and by the way, that Creed douche, he's been removed from the hospital, he assaulted Steve."

"Really?"

"Really, really."

"That's good news, here's hoping the good news continues to filter in."

"Positive thinking and it will," Andi says, ever the optimist.

Walking over to the nurses' station, I sit down and look at Lexi's file. Her recent blood work looks better, but she's still not out of the woods, her latest X-ray is uploaded and when I look at it, I smile. Her lungs are improving and we are about to move her from ICU to the children's ward.

The air around me crackles and I know she's back.

Looking up, I see Cress and even though she looks tired, she's still the sexiest woman I have ever seen. Her hair's up in a messy bun and she's wearing ass-hugging jeans and a simple black sweater. As usual, she makes a simple outfit look like catwalk couture.

Cress looks up and our gazes meet, she stops mid-step and stares back at me. I'm about to walk over to her, when Lexi is wheeled back in and our moment is over. I sit and watch as Cress races over to them. They wheel Lexi back into her room and what makes me smile, as she's wheeled past, I see her eyes are open and she's smiling. She sits up and tries to shout, "Prince Dr. Preston," her voice is quiet, but there's excitement in her eyes.

Standing up, I walk over to her room. "Princess Lexi, my favorite patient. How you feeling, Munchkin?"

"Better. Mommy says my medicine is working."

"It sure is. Sorry it took so long."

"It's okay. Can you stay?"

"Preston needs to get back to work, Munchkin, and you need to rest," Cress says without looking at or acknowledging me. It hurts but after my chat with Andi, I understand.

"Actually," Andi says from behind me as she enters the room, "now that you're better, we have a special ward for you. Do you want to see your new room, Lexi?"

"Yes, please." She looks to Cress. "And then we can watch Pony."

"Anything for you, Munchkin."

Stepping aside, I watch as Andi escorts Cress and Lexi to the children's ward with the help of an orderly. Looking up, I catch Cress staring at me. I smile but she quickly looks away. Standing in the now empty room, I spy another pony figurine on the rolling table and an idea forms. Racing out of the room, I head to the doctors' lounge to have some privacy and set my surprise up.

Walking into the lounge, Clay is lying on the bench and he's listening to music. "What song is that?" I ask him as I open my locker and grab out my laptop.

"It's "I Won't Give Up" by Jason Mraz."

Nodding my head, I smile. The words to this song sum up my feelings right now. I'm not giving up. I'm going to get Lexi better AND then I'm going to win Cress back. I'm not giving up, not ever when it comes to Cress and Lexi.

30   CRESS

Two days later, I wake up and like always, my eyes go straight to Lexi's bed and for the first time in almost a week I smile and it's a genuine smile. Her color is back to normal, she looks like Lexi again. The first thing I want to do is text Preston, but then I remember I can't. I was a total bitch to him and I broke us. Sighing, I realize I need to get used to not having him around anymore.

Lexi opens her eyes. "Mommy?"

"Yes, Munchkin?"

"I want toast."

Those three words mean everything to me. If she wants food, that means she's better. Preston did it, he fixed my little girl...and I pushed him away. "I'll see what I can do." Before I get a chance to get her some toast, the door to her room opens and a huge bouquet of balloons is delivered. It's filled with pink and purple love hearts, a Rainbow Dash 3D balloon and several round Pony gang ones. Then enters someone with a *My Little Pony* blanket that they place over the bed, a plush Rainbow Dash pony, and a basket of Pony figurines. Lexi grabs the plush pony and hugs it to her chest, it's just as big as her. The smile on her little face right now is priceless. Another person walks in behind with a lollipop bouquet, Lexi's eyes widen when she sees that. And lastly, someone hands me a venti-sized coffee from across the road.

"Holy duck," I say, as I take in the Pony explosion around us.

"Mommy, where did all of this come from?" Lexi asks me.

"I have no idea, Munchkin," I say, but I'm pretty sure I know where it all came from: Preston.

The hairs on the back of my neck stand on end, the air around me crackles and then I feel him behind me. My heart beats faster. My breathing becomes labored. It's been a few days since he's been this close to me and my body hasn't forgotten how he makes me feel.

"Morning," he says from behind me. The deep timbre of his voice warms me from the inside out.

"Prince Dr. Preston," Lexi beams. "Look what I got?" She holds up the pony and winces when she pulls on her IV.

Preston steps around me and over to her. "You okay, Munchkin?" His voice laced with concern; it pulls at my heartstrings. He really does care. Then I begin to wonder if I made a mistake. Did I overreact due to the situation with Lexi?

She nods. "I'm okay now," she says. "I haven't seened you much."

"I've been here. I've just been busy." He lifts his gaze to

mine. He smiles but it doesn't reach his eyes. He looks tired. His face is covered in a light beard, and he looks fucking hot if I'm honest. "You like your surprise?" he asks Lexi.

"You did all this?" Lexi asks him.

He nods at her. "Yep, I wanted to cheer you up." He looks over to me. "And you too," he says.

"I don't know what to say," I admit, a lump forming in the back of my throat because he did all of this, even though I pushed him away. But then I remember Lexi asking about him and I realize that, yes, he has been absent the last few days. Maybe he doesn't care after all, but then if he didn't care, he wouldn't have done all of this. I'm so confused right now.

"You don't need to say anything, Cress."

"You shouldn't have, Preston. We are…" I stop because I don't know how to finish that sentence. *What are we?* I broke what we were because I was scared, will we ever get back from that?

Turning away from him, I stare out into the corridor. "Cress," he says, touching my shoulder. "I just wanted—"

"No," I say, turning to face him. "You shouldn't have, Preston." When he looks at me, I know without a doubt: I made a mistake pushing him away and breaking us was the wrong choice. "We…I…I need a minute."

Racing out of the room, my eyes well with tears. Everything becomes blurry with each step I take. Turning the corner I bump into someone, they grip my shoulders to steady me. "Cress, are you okay?" Andi says, her voice laced with concern.

"I…he…Preston…I broke up with him."

"What did he do now?"

"Everything. He's kind and spoiling us. It's too much. I need him to leave us alone. We are over. I broke us. I can't do this. I—"

"Cress, that man loves you and Lexi with everything he has. I have never seen him like this before. He'll probably kick my ass for telling you this, but he's been here twenty-four seven for the last week. Checking in on Lexi and making sure she was getting the best possible treatment every chance he got. He'd hover and wait for you to leave, or he'd hide out at the nurses' station and watch her remotely."

"What?" I say, completely shocked at her revelation.

"You didn't know?"

"No," I shake my head and hold my hand to my chest. My heart rapidly beating at this revelation. "I never saw him."

"He's been here in the shadows. Watching. Hovering. Doing what he does best." She purses her lips. "This probably isn't my place to say, but give him another chance, Cress. What happened with Lexi was no one's fault. These things happen and generally without warning, especially in kids."

"But—"

"No buts, Cress. He's gutted you broke up with him, and he's pissed at himself that he didn't see this coming. You are the one for him, Cress, and I think, deep down, you know it too."

"I...I need air, excuse me." Stepping around her, I head toward the fire exit and race up the stairs to the roof. I found this place the other day when I needed air after breaking up with Preston.

Pushing the door open, I step out onto the rooftop. Walking over to the edge, I place down my coffee and stare out into the distance. My mind is racing a million miles an hour. The questions coming at me at light speed. Lowering my head down, I begin to cry as it all catches up with me and then it hits me: I made the biggest mistake of my life pushing away Dr. Knight.

# 31 CREED

This is turning out better than I anticipated. Cress broke up with the fucker and she's teetering on the edge. She'll be riding my cock, begging me for more very soon. It's a shame the kid pulled through, but if I play my cards right, I can make her hate Cressida. Or maybe Dr. Fuckhead will fuck up and miss something else, and then she'll die.

She races out of the room, tears pouring down her face. Dr. Fuckhead follows soon after, stopping at the nurses' station. When the coast is clear, I go into the squid's room. It looks like a fucking Pony explosion in here; balloons and toys are everywhere.

"What the fuck?" I snarl at the scene before me.

"Daddy Creed," she says. *Fuck, I hate it when she calls me that.*

"It's just fucking Creed, how many times do I have to tell you that?"

"Look what Prince Dr. Preston did for me," she excitedly says.

"Looks like he's trying to win you over for fucking up." She looks at me with a confused look. "You know you're in here because he fucked up and your mother is a whore."

"You are saying lots of naughty words."

"Joys of being an adult, kid. Where's Cressida?"

"She went for a walk, Prince Dr. Preston said she needed some air."

"Seems she doesn't care either."

"She does so. Mommy loves me."

"Really? That woman only knows how to love herself. She doesn't love you at all."

"Mommy loves me," she cries.

"If she did love you, she'd be here now. She clearly has more important things to do than sit here with you. Lexi, she doesn't love you."

"Mommy," Lexi cries, "does to love me."

"Shut the fuck up," I growl, reaching out, I pop a purple love heart balloon. The loud bang startling the squid and she begins to cry harder.

"For fuck's sake," I growl. "I'm your father, you need to listen to me and shut up. Stop with the tears." Anger courses through my veins. "Shut. The. Fuck. Up."

"I wish Prince Dr. Preston was my daddy, you're mean."

"And you whine too much. I'm your father, so you're stuck with me and if I have my way, you will be with me always."

"No," she cries, "I want Mommy."

"Tough shit. I want to see her and him suffer."

Deciding that my daughter is coming with me, I walk

toward the bed. I wish I could see the look on the bitch's face when she realizes that her precious daughter is gone.

"Sir," someone says from the doorway, "I'm going to have to ask you to leave."

Turning around I see the doctor's side whore. "Fuck off, lady, she's my daughter. I have a right to be here."

"That maybe so, but I will not tolerate someone speaking to a child like that. The whole ward just heard how you spoke to her. You've upset her and she's still recovering."

"Yeah, recovering 'cause both that bitch and fucker fucked up. I can speak to her however the fuck I want." I pause and glare at the woman before me, but she's one tough bitch and just glares at me. "Get the fuck out. NOW."

The bitch turns on her heel and walks out of the room, leaving me with a crying kid. "For fuck's sake. Stop crying, tears are for the weak. When you are mine, I will beat you tough just like my daddy did to me. No kid of mine is going to be a pussy."

"Sir," a deep male voice says from behind, "I'm going to have to ask you to leave."

"Make me," I snarl, no one tells me what to do.

"Last chance, sir, you need to leave now."

Turning around, I stare at him, this fucker looks like he means business and if I'm going to fuck Cress over, I cannot lose my shit now. "Fine," I huff. "I'll go but I'll be back." Without looking at the squid, I walk out of the room, shoving the guard in the shoulder as I walk past.

Entering the elevator, a plan formulates in my mind. Cress is going down…but first, a little fun.

32 CRESS

PICKING UP MY COFFEE, I TAKE A SIP, IT'S STONE-COLD. "Ugh," I whisper, "cold coffee, just another thing that's gone cold in my life."

Letting out a sigh, I continue to stare across the rooftops. I really wish I could call Ave right now, but she's still recovering and doesn't need this added to her worries. I know she'll kick my ass but she has enough on her plate at the moment.

The silence is broken when I hear my name, "Cress." Spinning around I come face-to-face with Preston. Worry etched on his gorgeous face.

"How did you find me here?"

"I will always find you, Cress, always." We silently stare at one another; again that déjà vu feeling washes over me. "When no one could find you, I just knew you'd be here because this where I come when I need to escape."

"It's beautiful up here."

"It sure is," he says, but his eyes are on me and I feel like he's referring to me and not the view.

We fall silent again and quietly stare at each other. The walls I previously put up begin to crumble and the regret at pushing him away festers within. My eyes well with tears when it hits me like a freight train; I want him. I need him. I love him. We need him in our life.

We.

Need.

Him.

But what if we've lost him? Because in haste, I pushed him away. That thought hurts like said freight train smashing into me, it utterly guts me that I pushed him away, I don't want that. I want Preston Knight in my and Lexi's life. "Preston—" I blubber.

He steps over to me and gently squeezes my upper arms. "Lexi is going to be fine...and so will we." *How did he know?* "Nothing will keep me from you. Not even an outburst when you thought your world was ending." He takes my cheeks in his palms and stares deep into my soul. "Cress, I'm never letting you go." He gently presses his mouth to mine and all the sadness, anger, fear, and unease I had evaporates as soon as his lips touch mine and I know, without a doubt, he's right.

I was falling for him from the moment I saw him and I want to fall even deeper in love with him. "I don't want you to let us go either, Preston. I'm going to jump in with both feet and give us my everything because you are my everything."

"Good, because me plus you and Lexi are my forever. My everything." He cups my cheek in his palm again. "I'm sorry I let you both down, but if you give me another chance, I'll never let that happen again. I was devastated at causing you this pain. When I lost you and Lexi, I thought my world was over. That little pony-loving princess has wormed her way deep into my heart, just like you have."

He wipes a tear from my cheek. "I love you, Preston," I whisper, leaning into his palm.

"I love you too, Cress. I never stopped and I never will."

Taking his cheeks in my hands, I press my lips to his. He slides his arms around my waist, pulling me into him. Wrapping my arms around his neck, I hold him tightly and pour everything into this kiss. He breaks the connection and rests his forehead against mine.

Everything is falling into place again. Lexi is getting better and I have Preston back in my life. Closing my eyes, I enjoy the moment.

Preston's pager goes off, he looks down and frowns "We need to head back down. Creed was just with Lexi and she's upset."

My eyes widen and my heart begins to race faster. "What?"

"He was just asked to leave."

My eyes widen, "We need to get back."

"Okay, let's go." He laces his fingers with mine and together, we head back inside and down to see Lexi.

When I step back into her room, my heart breaks. My little girl is sobbing and wrapped in Andi's arms. "Lexi, baby, what's wrong?"

"Daddy Creed is mean," she cries.

Fucking Creed, I think to myself as I race over to her bed. Andi stands up and I sit down and envelop Lexi into my arms. She cries and cries, it breaks my heart seeing her so upset.

Andi and Preston are quietly talking in the corner; from

the look on Preston's face he's as angry as I am right now. Andi leaves and Preston walks over to us.

"Hey, Princess Lexi. You okay, Munchkin?"

She nods her head but the tears keep coming. "Wanna tell Mommy and I what happened?" he asks, as he pulls a chair to the side of her bed.

"He popped a balloon and said Mommy doesn't love me and he swore. Lots."

"Munchkin, Mommy loves you to the moon and back. You know this, right?" She nods her head. "Creed is just having a bad day," I tell her, hoping that this will make her feel better.

"He said he wants to take me from you."

My eyes pop open, rage simmers in my blood that he would say this to her. Shaking my head, I hold her tighter to me. "I won't let that happen, Lex. I love you too much to let you go." Kissing her head, I look to Preston. He looks like I feel—ready to explode.

"I'm going to speak to security, make sure he isn't allowed back in."

"Thank you," I say, reaching my hand out to his. He takes my hand and squeezes it before bringing it to his lips and kissing my knuckles. He leans over and kisses Lexi's head before he walks out to speak to security.

Lying on the bed with Lexi, I hug her to me. Her body relaxes and I know she's fallen asleep. My mind plays over everything that has happened. I find myself smiling when I realize things are looking up again. Lexi is better, and Preston and I are back together. I came so close to losing both him and Lexi, now that I have them back, I'm going to hold on with both hands. I'm never letting them go, never.

33 PRESTON

LEXI HAS BEEN HEALTHY FOR SIX MONTHS NOW. IF I'M NOT AT the hospital, I'm with her and Cress. I'm watching her like a hawk, I will not miss her getting sick again. I'm in my office finalizing my proposal for the pediatric upgrade, the carrot offered to entice me to stay in Chicago. They weren't happy when I called them to decline their offer but by staying here, I get the job and the girls, making my life perfect.

I'm meeting with Dr. Jenkins tomorrow and if she agrees to my proposal, its going to be amazing to see my vision come to fruition.

My phone pings with a text, it's my brother. He and I have been playing phone tag for weeks now.

KEETON: *Hey, Doc. You free for dinner? I have news*
PRESTON: *Now's not a good time for dinner. What's the news?*

KEETON: *I'd rather tell you in person. Don't fret it's good news. Great news in fact.*
PRESTON: *Good news I can handle, maybe next week?*
KEETON: *Sounds good, let me know when and I'll set it up with Blair and Faith*
PRESTON: *Blair and Faith???*

What is my brother up to now? And why am I being invited to dinner with his business partner and some chick?

KEETON: *I'll explain over dinner. See you next week*

A few days later, Lexi, Cress, and I are in the blanket fort we made watching, you guessed it, *My Little Pony*. We are waiting for pizza to arrive when my phone rings and I smile when I see Keeton's name on the screen. "Hey, baby bro," I answer. I try and roll out of the fort but Lexi has a death grip on me so I lie back and get comfy.

"Are you alive? You didn't get back to me to arrange dinner," Keeton says.

"Duck, I totally forgot."

"Duck? Really?"

"Umm, yeah, I'm at my girlfriend's place and she has a kid.'

"Come again, girlfriend? With a kid?"

"Says the guy who wants me to have dinner with his business partner and meet some chick."

"Touché," he says, and I picture him nodding his head as he says this.

"So, are you going to tell me what's going on in your life?"

"Are you going to tell me about playing happy family?" he retorts back. I look to Lexi and Cress and realize I am, in fact, playing happy family but there's no playing. This is real life and I am one-hundred-percent committed to this family.

"You first," I counter.

"Of course, you'd say that. How about this weekend we all get together at your place? Enjoy the last of this good weather? Barbecue and swim?"

"Sounds great, let me just check with Cress."

"Pussy-whipped," he coughs down the line.

"Asshole," I whisper back.

"Prince Dr. Preston said a naughty word," Lexi says.

"He did, Mommy will punish him later." Cress winks at me and it goes straight to my cock.

"You guys free Sunday afternoon to meet my brother and his whatever they are?"

"Sounds good," Cress says, as Lexi asks, "Can we swim and have burgers?"

"Yes," Keeton shouts through the phone.

Cress and I laugh, "Of course, Munchkin."

Lifting the phone back to my ear. "So you heard that?"

"Yes, and tell Lexi she has great taste and Uncle K can't wait to meet her."

"You're a dick," I tell him.

"He said a naughty word again, Mommy."

"Double punishment is coming for him then."

"You're in trouble," Lexi singsongs.

"Thanks, bro, I'm in trouble 'cause of you."

"Happy to help. See you Sunday."

He hangs up and when I look over to Cress, her eyes are full of hunger and desire...I'm so looking forward to my punishment.

After pizza and more Pony episodes, I bathe and get Lexi into bed. Once she's asleep, I walk back into the kitchen, and notice Cress staring at her phone. "He text again?" I ask.

She lifts her gaze to mine, she smiles but it doesn't reach her eyes. "Yeah, but I did what you said, I deleted it straightaway." She walks over to me and wraps her arms around my waist and rests her head on my chest.

"Thank you," she murmurs.

"What are you thanking me for?"

"For being you. For loving me and Lexi like you do."

"I do love you both, with all my heart, Cress." She lifts her gaze to mine and smiles, this time it reaches her eyes. She presses her lips to mine and when she pulls back, her eyes are full of hunger and desire. Taking her hand, I lead her into her bedroom.

She pulls away. "I just need some water, give me a minute."

Nodding my head, I watch as she walks back into the kitchen, turning around I walk into her bedroom and remove my shirt and pants, leaving me in my boxers. I sit on the edge of the bed and fall back to the mattress, I'm shattered and cannot wait to crawl into bed with Cress. A throat clearing from the doorway causes my head to raise and when I look up my eyes bug out of my head.

Cress is leaning against the doorframe in the sexiest piece of lingerie I have ever seen. She's wearing silky black panties that match a sexy as fuck white satin bra adorned with black lace, that flows into a black mesh that stops just at her panty line. "Fuck me, Cress. You are the sexiest woman alive."

From behind her back, she has an open bottle of bubbly

in one hand and a plate of chocolate-coated strawberries in the other. "We need to celebrate."

"What are we celebrating?"

"There's lots to celebrate, Dr. Knight."

"Come here," I growl.

Cress pushes off the doorframe and saunters over to me. Swishing her hips side to side as she goes. She places the plate of strawberries onto the bedside table and brings the bottle to her lips and drinks. She leans down and presses her lips to me, the bubbly going from her mouth to mine. Some spills down her chin and neck. Leaning forward, I lick down her throat and chest, lapping up the spilt bubbly.

Wrapping my arms around her waist, she straddles my thighs and stares at me. The air in the room is heated and thick with desire. Taking the bottle from her, I take a sip. Then I lift it up and pour some across her chest. Pulling her closer to me, I lick the cold liquid from her skin, goosebumps breaking out across her chest. Sucking her nipple through the material, it pebbles and hardens. Licking across her chest, I do the same to the other one. Her head drops back and I continue to lick and suck her chest. She circles her hips on my lap and cries out when she can't rub herself on me.

"Patience, my dear," I mumble against her skin.

"Fuck patience, I want your cock in me now," she mewls, grinding herself on my leg. She is soaked.

"Well, I want to savor this sexy as fuck outfit you have on," I taunt, squeezing her ass and pulling her back up so she can't rub herself on me anymore.

Gripping my cheeks, she stares intently at me. "Preston, I will wear this every day for a week, just fuck me now."

Staring back at her, I slam my lips to hers and fuck her mouth with my tongue. She moans into my mouth. My cock is rock-hard and I'm ready to fuck her, but I want to tease her a little longer. I increase my grip on her ass and gently slide her back and forth on my leg.

"Please, Preston," she begs.

Gripping the edge of her panties, I break our kiss. "I hope you aren't fond of these panties," I say before I tear them off her, the flimsy material disintegrating at the force. Before she can protest, I flip her on to her back, remove my briefs, and push inside her.

Her pussy welcomes my cock, hugging it tight. Pushing my hips, I thrust in and out of her. Sitting up, I lift her leg over my shoulder and continue to slide in and out of her. Her eyes are closed, her mouth open. She moans and groans in the sexiest way as I fuck her hard.

She reaches up, pulls down the cup of her teddy and plays with her breasts. "Cress, that is the sexiest thing I have ever seen."

Her eyes open and we stare at one another as I continue to pump in and out of her. She slides her hands between us and rubs her clit. Her walls tighten around me and together we explode. Our bodies shudder as we give ourselves over to the pleasure.

Lowering her leg. I pull out and stare down at her. She looks gorgeous with her flushed cheeks and chest glowing from her orgasm. Climbing onto the bed, she snuggles into my side, and we drift off to sleep wrapped in each other's arms.

The next day, I head to the hospital to see Dr. Jenkins. She agreed to everything in my proposal. I'm glad I turned down Boston, my life is here with Lexi and Cress. I've finished up another meeting and I'm heading to my car, looking forward to getting home to my girls. The elevator stops and Flynn hops in. "Hey," I say, noticing the bags under his eyes, "you finishing or starting?"

"Just finished. You?"

"Same." My phone rings as we enter the parking garage, I smile when I see it's Momma Cress. I slide to answer and before I say anything she cries, "Preston, we have a problem."

34 CRESS

Mom stopped by and asked to take Lexi for ice cream, wanting a few hours to myself I happily obliged. Taking the opportunity, I change from my pajamas into a black-and-white blouse and my black capris. Heading to the mall, I treat myself to a quiet coffee. My phone pings with a text and I freeze like I always do at the moment when I hear that sound. Creed is still text taunting me but I no longer read them, I delete them, but much to my delight, I see it's from Ave.

> **AVERY:** *Guess what?*
> **CRESS:** *What?*
> **AVERY:** *Bay is getting released next month.*

Rolling my eyes, I shake my head. Baylor Evans is the polar opposite of my best friend, even more so now that she has a criminal record. Ave assures me she's changed, but I personally think, *once a bitch, always a bitch.*

CRESS: *That's great news. Wanna meet for coffee?*
AVERY: *I'd love to, but Flynn and I are busy this
afternoon*

I read that as code for 'we are going to fuck like
rabbits.'

CRESS: *Fine, but we need to do drinks soon. Feels
like it's been forever since I've seen you*
AVERY: *Sounds good…maybe you will finally spill
the deets on you and a Channing Tatum look-alike
doctor that you seem to be spending a lot of
time with*

A laugh escapes at that. I'm not sure why I haven't
come out and specifically told her about Preston and me.
She's not dumb, or blind, but at the same time she hasn't
asked, and we really haven't seen each other much in the
last few months. Since Lexi got sick, she's been my main
focus and since Ave moved in with Flynn, she's been in the
honeymoon phase.

CRESS: *Tell me when and where for drinks, and I will
bring ALL the gossip.*
AVERY: *It's a date…Jelember work for you?*
CRESS: *Hahaha, that sounds about right. When did
we get so busy that we have to resort to text
messages to communicate?*
AVERY: *When we got old*
CRESS: *Hey, I'm not old…you're old*
AVERY: *I'm ending this before you hurt my feelings.
Catch up soon.*
AVERY: *Love your 'old' face **stick out tongue emoji***

CRESS: *Love your 'old' face too. See you soon, raccoon*

Clearly Preston is rubbing off on me when I read back that last message. Shaking my head, I finish my coffee and head back home. Stopping at the store, I grab a few things to start marinating the chicken for the barbecue tomorrow. I'm excited and nervous to be meeting Preston's brother and partners. Keeton, Preston's brother is in a throuple with Blair and Faith. I've never met anyone in a throuple, so I'm intrigued to hear and see how it works.

Realizing I left a bag in the car, I head back outside. I'm leaning into the back seat when I'm pulled by my hair from the car and spun around. "You fucking bitch," he snarls.

"Creed—" I don't get to finish that sentence because he slams my head into the side of the car. It hurts like a bitch. I see black-and-white stars and my hearing is now fuzzy, it sounds like I'm underwater. Creed is blurry. I blink rapidly and my sight returns. Creed is red in the face, I can see his lips moving but I still can't hear properly.

He grabs me by the throat and squeezes. Lifting my hands, I try to pry him off me but I'm not as strong as him. Fear bubbles inside of me, without thinking, I lift my leg and knee him in the balls. As soon as I do it, I realize it's a mistake because his face becomes even more enraged. "Ohh, you've done it now, bitch." He grips my hair, the follicles pulling from the force. He drags me up the front path and inside. I try to scream out but my voice is hoarse from him squeezing my neck.

He opens the screen door and throws me inside. Landing on my hands and knees, I flinch at the pain. He grabs me by my shoulders and flips me over. He straddles my waist, grabs my hands and pulls them above my head. He pins them down with one hand and rests the other next to my head. I stare up at him and I freeze, I have never seen Creed like this before.

My breathing is coming in short fast bursts. My heart is rapidly beating, it feels like it will burst through my chest. "Creed, please," I beg.

"I love it when you beg. Beg me to fuck you. Beg me, Babydoll. Beg me for my cock."

"Please, Creed," I cry. "Please don't hurt me."

"I'm not going to hurt you, Babydoll, I'm going to fuck you like you've never been fucked before, and then you are going to come with me and we will live together just like we used too."

"You are delusional. I'm not going anywhere with you."

"It's not like you have a choice in the matter. Now, do you want my cock in your ass? Mouth? Or cunt first?"

Shaking my head side to side, I try to wriggle free but it's no use. He's got me pinned down. He grips my chin tightly and forces me to look up at him. I close my eyes tight, ever so thankful that Lexi isn't here right now.

"Open your eyes, slut. I want to see the look in them when I sink myself inside of you."

Again I shake my head side to side. He slaps me hard across the cheek, my eyes fly open. My cheek stinging from the slap. My eyes well with tears. "Please, Creed." I beg him again. "Please don't do this."

He roughly grabs my breast, squeezing and pressing down on my chest. I gasp when he tears at my blouse and rips at the cup of my bra, then lowers his head and roughly bites me. I scream, pain tearing through my breast. He lifts his head and stares down at me. I've never seen a more sinister look on his face. He slides his hand down my stomach. I close my eyes waiting for him to slip under the waistband of my pants, but it doesn't come. Someone pulls Creed off me.

Opening my eyes, I see Flynn standing in the doorway. Preston is next to me, punching Creed in the face over and over. "Stop," I try to shout but my voice is hoarse. "Stop him!" I yell at Flynn.

Flynn steps to Preston and shouts. "Cress needs you, man." This causes Preston to pause mid-swing. He looks over to me and when our gazes connect, his eyes widen. He punches Creed once more and shuffles over to me. He takes me into his arms, I wrap mine around his waist, and I cry into his embrace.

Flynn has his foot pressing Creed's chest, holding him down. He has his phone to his ear, speaking to the authorities. Everything is muffled as I hold on to Preston and continue to cry.

Soon, my house is full with police officers and EMTs. The paramedic gives me the all clear and Preston agrees to watch over me, therefore saving me a trip to the hospital. Between Ave and Lexi in the last six months, I'm over hospitals.

Everyone has left and finally it's just Preston and me. We are sitting on the sofa when the front door opens, I look up and see Mom and Lexi walk in. "Hey, Munchkin, did you have fun with Nanna?"

"Yes. Not only did I get ice cream but I got to see a movie too."

"Wow, aren't you lucky."

It seems Mom was on her way back here when she saw the altercation with Creed, she kept driving and called Preston. Preston told her to keep Lexi away until she heard from him or me. I'm thankful Mom drove past when she did because who knows what would have happened otherwise.

Focusing on Lexi, I look around the room and smile. I have the three most important people in my life with me and after today, Creed will never be able to hurt or taunt us again. He was arrested for assault and will be behind bars for the foreseeable future. Apparently that agent who stopped by a few weeks back was building a case and this will add to that. Creed is going to be behind bars for a very long time to come. Lexi and I can now live life happy and carefree, with Preston.

35 PRESTON

…six weeks later

I'M VISITING MY MENTOR, DR. TARA OLE, IN IDAHO. SHE LEFT the big city when she retired and now consults at the local hospital here. I'm visiting, as I want to bounce some ideas off her before I present them to Dr. Jenkins. I officially start my new role next month, and we are going to transform our pediatric wing into the best in the country, sorry Boston. My team and I are going to make Western General THE top pediatric hospital in the country; again sorry not sorry, Boston. Dr. Jenkins has already approved stage one, but with Dr. Ole's help, I'm going to propose a stage two, really elevating the hospital.

It's been great seeing her again but I can't wait to get back to Chicago to see Cress and Lexi. I miss them both dearly, that little girl has wormed her way into my heart. Much like her mother has, if things go sour with Cress and me, I'll be devastated not seeing the Pony-obsessed little munchkin.

Today I'm assisting in the ER, as they are short-staffed. It's crazy busy. My next case is a little boy with a fractured arm; it will be an easy one to wrap up my time here. It has been great catching up with Dr. Ole. She has played a major part in my career. Without her, I wouldn't be half the doctor I am today.

Pulling the curtain back, I look up from the chart in my hand. "I'm Dr. Knight, seems our lil' slugger here has a fractured wrist." Clipping the X-ray up on to the light box, I step next to Dad and notice him staring at it too. He turns his head, and gazes at his partner. "It's a clean break, Autumn, he'll be fine," he says, confirming my suspicion that he too is a doctor.

"Your husband is correct," I agree, "Oliver's break is a clean one."

"He's not my dad," Oliver says from the bed.

"My mistake." My eyes dart between the three of them, there's clearly some tension between them, and I can't help but check out the woman before me. She is gorgeous: blue eyes, blonde hair, killer body but she has nothing on my Cress.

"Dr. Griffin Steel," he says, stretching out his hand to me.

"Dr. Preston Knight, visiting from Chicago." He shakes my hand, squeezing tightly, unofficially telling me to back the hell off.

His eyes widen, and then I realize he's heard of me before. Nodding my head, I smile. "Pleasure to meet a fellow colleague."

He ignores me and focuses on the woman again,

"Autumn, seems Ollie here has the best pediatric specialist in the midwest on his case."

"How do you know he's the best?" she questions him.

"Preston Knight of Western General is the best in his field. Boston Children's Hospital wanted him to head their pediatric department, but he chose to stay at Western General and head up their new pediatric department instead. It caused quite the stir when he turned down the top job in Boston."

"What can I say, I don't like to conform to what's expected of me."

"So the rumors are true then?"

I shrug my shoulders and wink, seems the rumor about me turning down Boston is making the rounds, that's one of the reasons I came here to see Tara. I needed her to reassure me that I made the right decision. Wanting to change the topic, I look to Oliver. "So, Oliver, from here, we will get you cast up and then you can head home. I don't need to go through the instructions, as I'm sure Dr. Steel here will look after you."

"We don't need Griffin's help," Oliver's mom snaps. "Can you please tell me what I need to do?"

"Of course."

As I explain this to Autumn, I notice Griffin intently watching her. There's some major tension, sexual tension, between the two of them.

As soon as Ollie's cast has set, I drop off the discharge papers and watch them leave. From the outside, they look like a loving family but from the brief time I was with them, I know that's not the case. My phone buzzes in my pocket, removing it, I smile when I see it's from Cress. Sliding it open, I read.

CRESS: *Hey, Doc. When do you get back?*

PRESTON: *Hey, sexy lady. Will be back tomorrow*

CRESS: *Up for dinner and a sleepover? Mom and Lexi are having a sleepover so I want one too*

PRESTON: *Will this be a naked kind of sleepover?*

CRESS: *Is there any other kind?*

CRESS: *Your place or mine?*

PRESTON: *Can we do mine? I have to be at the hospital the day after for an early shift*

CRESS: *I will definitely be doing you and I don't care where we sleep…not that there will be much sleeping at this sleepover*

PRESTON: *Down, girl, I can't be sporting a boner right now, I'm in the middle of the ER*

CRESS: *I know the best medicine for that and I will happily administer it tomorrow **wink wink***

PRESTON: *Dammit, Cress. Your ass is mine when I get home*

CRESS: *Promise?*

PRESTON: *Fuuuuck, woman, I'm going now before I lose my medical license. I'll message you when I get home*

CRESS: *I can pick you up, if you like?*

PRESTON: *You'd do that?*

CRESS: *I'd do you **wink** and yes, I'd love to. Text me your flight details*

PRESTON: *Will do when I get back to the hotel. See you tomorrow, sexy lady*

CRESS: *Later, Doc. Love you **wink emoji***

PRESTON: *'Til then, penguin **kiss emoji***

The flight home is uneventful and we even land early. Walking out, I'm focused on my phone and I'm not watching where I'm walking and bump into someone's back. They spin around and it's Cress. "Cress, Love, I'm so sorry."

"It's fine. I shouldn't have stopped in the middle of the walkway. I was flustered 'cause your flight got in early and I wanted to be at the gate when you landed."

"Aww, did you miss me?"

"Maybe," she nonchalantly says. She stares at me and the hunger in her gaze has my cock twitching in my pants.

Wrapping my arms around her, I pull her to me and whisper into her ear, "Let's get you back to my place, I believe we have a naked sleepover to get to."

"Let's go." She slips her hand between us, squeezes my dick, winks, turns around, and walks away from me. Swinging her hips seductively with each step she takes toward the exit...I can't wait to get home.

36 CRESS

PRESTON AND I HAVE AN AMAZING SLEEPOVER, LIKE WE always do. That man knows how to bring my body alive, I don't think I've ever orgasmed as intensely as I do with him. Our bodies fit together perfectly, it's like we were destined to meet. He's the other half of me that was missing, when I'm with him, I'm whole and complete. Like that movie line, "He completes me."

Waking up in his arms is my most favorite way to start my day, I wish we could do it every day, but it's too soon to even think about moving in together. We haven't even been a couple for twelve months yet.

The morning flies by and before I know it, I'm off to school to get Lexi. When I pick her up, she's quiet and not her usual bubbly self. "What's wrong, Munchkin?"

"It's the daddy/daughter dance and I don't got a daddy now." My heart breaks at her words.

"I'm sure Preston would take you."

"But he's not my daddy."

"Ohh, Munchkin, come here." I drop down to my knees and I envelop her in my arms. "How about you ask him? I'm sure he'd love to go as your daddy."

"I wish he was my daddy," she sadly says.

"I do too, baby."

The car trip home is quiet today. I play Lexi's words over and over in my head, I too wish Preston was her daddy. When we get home, she heads straight to her bedroom. Making a chocolate milk, I grab some cookies and head down to her room. Knocking on her door, I step inside and find her on the floor playing with her ponies.

"Thought you might like a choccie milk and some cookies."

"Thanks, Mommy," she says.

"And we need to come up with a plan on how you are going to ask Preston to the dance."

"But he's not my daddy."

"Daddy is just a name. You may not call Preston Daddy, but I'm pretty sure he loves you like a daddy does."

"Really?"

"Yep. Now, let's come up with a plan."

Over cookies and milk, Lexi and I devise a plan.

The slamming of a car door outside startles me but at the same time, I smile, knowing what's about to happen. "Lexi, he's here," I shout from my spot on the sofa.

"I'm ready," she yells back.

Preston knocks. "Avon calling," he singsongs as he enters.

"You're a dork," I tell him.

"A dork who you love," he says, as he leans over the back of the sofa and kisses me. "Where's Lex?" he asks, looking around the room for her.

"She's in her room, she has something to ask you."

"Okay." He nods and walks down the hallway.

Leaning over the edge of the sofa, I try to peek down but I can't see or hear anything. The anticipation is killing me.

A few moments later, they both return. Lexi is in the outfit she picked, the princess dress Preston gave her a few months back, and she's holding his hand. The sight is adorable and has my ovaries doing summersaults.

"Mommy, Preston is going to be my daddy."

"That's great, baby."

"And you are going to be his queen."

Scrunching my face up in confusion, I look between the two of them. Lexi nudges Preston and he steps over to me, he drops down to one knee and takes my hand in his. "Cress, you and Lexi both mean the world to me. I already think of her as my daughter, I have from the first time I met her. You stole my heart the night we met and I'm pretty sure, I stole yours too." My eyes well with tears. "Lexi is right, I'm going to be her daddy because I want you to become my wife." From his pocket, he pulls out Lexi's plastic ruby princess ring. "Cressida Rachel Bayliss, will you marry me?"

Nodding my head, I blubber, "Yes, yes I'll marry you."

Gripping my cheeks in his hands, he presses his lips to mine and kisses me, cementing our engagement. He pulls back and I stare into his green eyes, they are shining brightly right now. "I love you, Preston."

"I love you too, Cress."

"I love my mommy and daddy," Lexi says from beside us.

Looking over to her, I smile. "Did you know, Munchkin?"

She nods her head. "When I asked him to be my daddy, he asked me if I can be his daughter and you his queen."

Looking to Preston, I smile. My heart is so full right now. I have my daughter and I have my prince. Falling for Dr. Knight was the best decision I ever made, right after saying yes to becoming Mrs. Preston Knight.

EPILOGUE

…two years later

"Preston, get me drugs. Get me every fucking drug there is. It hurts so much."

"Cress, Love, I wish I could but you are too far along now," he says, wiping my forehead with a wet cloth.

I've been in labor for forty-two hours now, I'm ready for this baby to be out but mini Preston wants to stay inside. He's stubborn like his father. I don't actually know if it's a boy or not, but he's being an asshole right now… just like his father, who won't get me the good drugs. "What's the point in being married to a doctor if he won't give me the good stuff when I'm in labor?"

"It's nice to know you are only with me for my access to the good drugs."

"Ohh shit!" I scream as another contraction hits. It passes quickly, I'm panting heavily. "Preston," I cry, "I'm sorry I'm a bitch."

"It's fine, Love. You are doing great, we are so close to meeting our little princess."

"Prince," I say, as another contraction hits. "I need to push," I shout.

Dr. Jenkins looks up from between my thighs, and nods. "Yes, Cressida, it's time."

"It's fucking Cress," I growl at her, and I really shouldn't because she's doing me a favor delivering bub number two. The chief doesn't usually deliver babies but I managed to sweet talk her into doing this for Preston and I. The next contraction hits. I push and scream squeezing Preston's hand tightly in mine.

"I see the head. Cress, on the next one, I want you to push hard," she says, her eyes focused between my thighs.

Nodding my head, I close my eyes and push and scream with everything I have. The room goes quiet and then baby Knight lets out a cry. It's the most beautiful sound in the world.

"You did it, Cress," Preston says, kissing me on the lips. "We have a baby—"

"—girl."

"We have a Pepper," I cry.

"Do you want to do the honors, Dad?" Dr. Jenkins asks.

Preston looks to me and I nod. Looking down I watch as he cuts the cord and then Dr. Jenkins hands me our daughter. Taking her into my arms, my eyes well with tears. "Hi, Pepper. I'm your mommy and this is your daddy. Your big sister, Lexi, cannot wait to meet you, and neither can your cousins, Marvin and Marshall."

"And in nine months, she'll have another cousin to play with."

"Ave is pregnant?" I question.

Preston shakes his head. "No, Keet, Blair, and Faith are expecting."

"Oh My God, that's amazing. "Who's the daddy?"

He shrugs. "Both of them, I guess."

"That's amazing. Babies all round."

After I'm stitched back up, I'm wheeled back to my room. Mom and Lexi are waiting, Lexi's face lights up when she sees me. "Where's my sister?" she asks.

"How did you know it was a girl?"

"'Cause I asked Santa for a baby sister last year."

The door opens, and Preston enters, pushing the bassinet with Pepper in it. Lexi races over and stares down at her.

"Why's her head all squished?"

Mom, Preston, and I all laugh. "Lexi, your head was like that when you were born too," Preston says, pulling her into his side as they stare down at Pepper.

"Really?"

"Yep, it's true."

"Can I hold her?"

"Mom needs to feed her first, and then you can."

Preston reaches in, lifts Pepper up, and holds her to his chest. Seeing him with our little girl fills my heart with so much joy. He steps to the bed and hands Pepper to me. "Hey, Munchkin," I whisper, kissing her on the head before I start feeding her. It all comes back to me, as if it was just yesterday that I was doing this with Lexi for the first time.

Preston is standing with Lexi and Mom; he must feel me staring at him. He looks over his shoulder at me. Our eyes connect and that déjà vu moment hits me. I'm transported back to when Lexi was born. Dr. Jenkins came in for rounds and a doctor caught my eye. We had a moment, just like this one. It was intense. It was electric. It was perfect, his gaze penetrated deep into my soul; just like it does when Preston stares at me. And it hits me, Preston was that doctor. "It was you," I say.

"Who was who?" Mom asks.

"It was Preston."

"What was Preston?" Mom asks, as Preston says, "What did I do?"

"When I had Lexi, you were there. You were on rounds with Dr. Jenkins, we had a moment and then you left."

Preston stares at me and I see the moment he remembers too. "Oh My God."

He walks across the room and kisses me on the forehead. After all these years, I finally found my prince, and he happened to be the one I'd been dreaming about all these years. That explains why falling for Dr. Knight was so easy, our love story began before either of us knew it.

THE END!

She's the twin you love to hate. Will Baylor get her HEA and redeem herself?
Find out late 2020, preorder Falling for Agent Cox today.

There's a fine line between love and hate.
A love fueled from hate is the strongest of them all.

BAYLOR
My life hasn't gone as I planned, but it's all my doing.
I'm given a second chance.
But I didn't count on him—Agent Corey Cox.
He's on the straight and narrow, abiding by the rules.
He calms my inner beast and makes me want to be a better person.
When my past reappears, that wildness inside sparks to life again.
Is his love enough to stop me turning my back on everything I've worked so hard for?

COREY
I live my life by the book.
Being an agent is everything to me.
The lines are never blurred.
Until her—Baylor Evans.
She's wild, carefree, and marches to the beat of her own drum.
She brings out a side to me I never knew existed.

But it all implodes, when I'm faced with an impossible decision.
Either way I lose.

To see how Avery and Flynn got together, grab Falling for Dr. Kelly.
It's available to buy now.

Every force has an equal and opposite attraction.
Love being the most volatile of them all.

AVERY
My life is anything but boring.
So what if I'm an introvert and prefer to focus on my career?
I was fine.
Until I met him—Flynn Kelly.
The doctor with the sexy Irish accent.
I thought we were unbreakable, until someone close hurts me in an unimaginable way.
Can two opposites fight the laws of attraction or will it end up tearing us apart?

FLYNN
I work hard, and play even harder.
When it came to women, I could have anyone I want.
Until I met her—Avery Evans.
She's quiet, shy, and everything I'm not.
But we're drawn together like magnets, sparking each other to life.
When the unthinkable happens, our differences really show.
Is our attraction about to sizzle and flame out? Only time will tell.

PLAYLIST

Breakeven – The script
You Found Me – The Fray
Duck Tales – main theme – Geek Music
Let Her Go – Passenger
I Won't Give Up – Jason Mraz
Forever and Always – Parachute
She Will Be Loved – Maroon 5
Not Over You – Gavin DeGraw
Closer – Nine Inch Nails
SexyBack (feat. Timberland) – Justin Timberlake
Pony – Ginuwine
Torn – Natalie Imbruglia
Walking Away – Craig David
My Little Pony theme song – Twilight Sparkle
Bleeding Love – Leona Lewis
I'm Yours – Jason Mraz
Someone Like You – Adele
Girls Like You – Maroon 5
What About Us – P!nk
Heathens – Twenty One Pilots

Let You Down – NF

Letters from the Sky – Civil Twilight

I Will Wait – Mumford & Sons

Touch Me (I Want your body) – Samantha Fox

All of Me – John Legend

How to Save a Life – The Fray

You And Me – Lifehouse

Shake it Off – Taylor Swift

Hands to Myself – Selena Gomez

For the First Time – The Script

Secrets – OneRepublic

Lips of an Angel – Hinder

All The Right Moves – OneRepublic

Cheap Thrills – Sia

You're The One That I Want – Loving Caliber

This playlist can be found on Spotify.

ACKNOWLEDGMENTS

To, **my family; Troy, Piper** and **Kade.** You three are my rocks, my loveable pains in the butt. You are my every-thing. Love you all to the moon and back XoXoX

Andi, thank you isn't enough for all that you did. You helped me bring Preston to life and turn him into the suave sweet/dirty talking doctor that he is. Preston is one hundred percent yours.

My beta babes; **Andi, Jenny, Stefanie** and **Tara;** thank you ladies once again for reading my book baby and giving me your opinions and feedback. You gals helped make this book what it is.

My editor, **Karen**, from **Barren Acres Editing;** I'm running out of things to say. You're not only my editor, but you're also a great friend; why do you live so far away? Thank you, once again for helping me turn my book baby from a pile of crap into a beautiful book baby.

My cover designer, **Kristie** from **Vanilla Lily Designs**. As soon as I saw this cover, I knew it was Preston and Cress. Thank you once again for a gorgeous cover.

Thank you to **Lana** and **Margaret** for checking my I's

are dotted and my T's are crossed. No matter how many times I read it, I always miss a few.

To the following authors; **Chloe Renee, Stefanie Jenkins, Renee Linda, Tara Lee, Alley Ciz, Cass Fowler;** thank you for your support, encouragement and writing sprints. Without you guys, I'd be a mess in the corner drinking wine from my coffee mug.

And finally **you, my readers**; thank you for the kind words that you message me with each release. 9 out of 10 times, these arrive just when I need a pick me up and they always do. From the bottom of my heart, thank you for supporting me and my books.

Cheers,

Dana Xo

PS. I cannot wait to get messages from you after reading Falling for Dr. Knight. I'm sure there will be messages of love and hate; I'm sorry for Creed but without him and his Dickwad ways, it would have been a super boring story.

The Unexpected Letter

The Unexpected Package

The Unexpected Connection

STAND ALONES

Out of Nowhere

Antecedent

Seven Nights

Falling for Dr. Kelly, a Falling novel

Falling for Dr. Knight, a Falling novel

Falling for Agent Cox, a Falling novel - COMING SOON

The Rule Breaker anthology

In the Dark of Night anthology

Love is Contagious, a charity anthology

Doc Steel

FACEBOOK ~ INSTAGRAM ~ BOOKBUB

GOODREADS ~ WEBSITE

dlgallieauthor@outlook.com

Sign up to my newsletter